Katie tried [illegible]
words, on the anger she had [illegible]ier.
But it was gone. All she could think about was his touch, his body so close to hers. She tried to respond. To protest that what she needed was her life back, but all the fight in her was gone. It wasn't fighting that she was thinking about now. Instead, it was the desire that had become a hot fire in her lower belly.

What would he do if she moved closer? If she reached up with her lips and touched his?

Her hand went up and pressed against his chest before she could stop it. His heart beat a fast rhythm against her palm as hers did when he covered her hand with his own.

"Do you feel it?" she asked him.

What was she doing? This wasn't her. She didn't approach men. Not like this. Instead, she waited until they showed an interest in her before expressing her own.

"Katie, I… Yes, if you mean do I want to take you in my arms and kiss you, and more, right now? Yes."

Dear Reader,

Have you ever met a stranger with whom you found yourself discussing things that you didn't feel comfortable discussing with your family and friends? This recently happened to me and it is exactly what happens after registered nurse Katie McGee meets coworker and new neighbor paramedic Dylan Maddox.

After recovering from a gunshot wound she received while trying to save her patient, Katie is only too happy to leave New York City and her meddling brothers behind for a few weeks. But the peace and quiet that she expects to find isn't possible as Dylan and his daughter, Violet, take it upon themselves to welcome her to the island of Key West.

While not a traditional friends to lovers story, I hope you will enjoy my new-friends to lovers story as these two share their devotion for their job on their helicopter crew while their mutual trust and attraction takes them on an adventurous journey to their happily-ever-after.

Best wishes,

Deanne

FLORIDA FLING WITH THE SINGLE DAD

DEANNE ANDERS

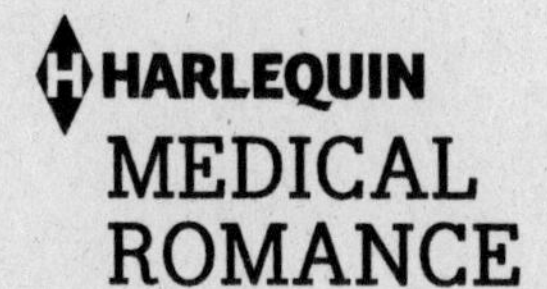

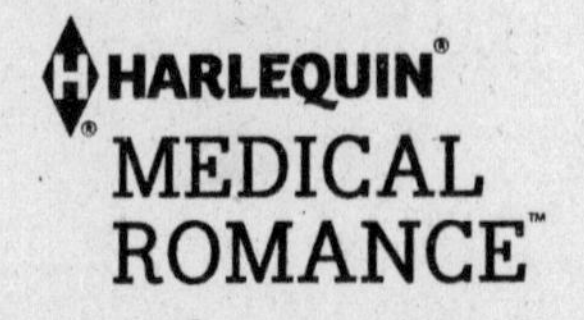

ISBN-13: 978-1-335-40915-7

Florida Fling with the Single Dad

This edition published by arrangement with Harlequin Books S.A.

For questions and comments about the quality of this book, please contact us at CustomerService@Harlequin.com.

Harlequin Enterprises ULC
22 Adelaide St. West, 41st Floor
Toronto, Ontario M5H 4E3, Canada
www.Harlequin.com

Printed in U.S.A.

Deanne Anders was reading romance while her friends were still reading Nancy Drew, and she knew she'd hit the jackpot when she found a shelf of Harlequin Presents in her local library. Years later she discovered the fun of writing her own. Deanne lives in Florida, with her husband and their spoiled Pomeranian. During the day she works as a nursing supervisor. With her love of everything medical and romance, writing for Harlequin Medical Romance is a dream come true.

Books by Deanne Anders

Harlequin Medical Romance

From Midwife to Mommy
The Surgeon's Baby Bombshell
Stolen Kiss with the Single Mom
Sarah and the Single Dad
The Neurosurgeon's Unexpected Family
December Reunion in Central Park

Visit the Author Profile page at Harlequin.com.

This book is dedicated to all the courageous first responders, including our helicopter crews, who put themselves in danger daily as they work to save the lives of strangers.

Praise for
Deanne Anders

"This story captivated me. I enjoyed every moment. This is a great example of a medical romance. Deanne Anders is an amazing writer!"

—*Goodreads* on *The Surgeon's Baby Bombshell*

CHAPTER ONE

KATIE MCGEE STARED at the sign reading Flight Crew as she knocked on the door of the small modular building located beside a large helipad that contained a blue-and-gold medevac helicopter. Was she ready for this? Absolutely not. Did she have a choice? The answer to that was exactly the same. But she'd promised Alex that she would help him out and she always kept her promises.

Oh, she could have turned him down, and at first she had started to because she'd assumed it was just another of his ploys to get her to come to Key West, but he had sounded so stressed when he'd called that she had known immediately something was up and he really did need her.

So after four days of driving she was finally on the island her friend now called home. And after everything that had happened in the last six months, she was lucky she'd been given this opportunity to help her friend out. She could still be in the hospital recuperating from her injury. Or she could even be dead.

But she'd survived. And now, even though there were a lot of her coworkers who had insinuated she might not be ready to get back out on the job of flight nurse, she'd proven to both them and her family that she was just as capable now as she had been before the shooting.

So why did she feel so nervous? Maybe because it was the first time in her life that she was all alone this far away from home?

Giving up on someone coming to the door, she opened it. The smell of burnt popcorn filled her nose. It seemed at least one person was awake and moving around in the quiet building.

Stepping through the door, she noticed the oversize gray couch and the big screen TV hanging on the back wall of the large open room. It was the same in all of Heli-Care operations: the bigger the TV, the happier the crew.

She wasn't surprised to see that the room was empty. Most flight crew shifts were twenty-four hours long, so it wouldn't be unusual for the crew to be catching a nap in their rooms. If she was lucky, the assistant manager would be available to set up the required new location orientation this morning and she could be on her way. After the drive from New York, she just wanted to get moved into the rental Alex had procured for the next two months, unpack her bags and take a long, cool shower.

Letting her offended nose lead her, she walked through an open doorway and entered a small galley kitchen. A tall man stood at a trash can, emptying out a burnt paper bag that was obviously the source of the smell now overwhelming the small room. Seeing a window over the sink, she hurried over to open it. It didn't budge. Two strong hands joined hers and together they pushed up the heavy window. Light green eyes with flecks of gold met hers. Unable to look away, she stood frozen in place within the circle of this man's arms.

"Hello," the man said, "you must be Katie."

His face close to hers, she studied the chiseled cheekbones and square jaw with just enough growth that there was no doubt it was intentional. His light brown curly hair framed a face that was meant for the magazines. But it was the eyes that mesmerized her. They seemed to look deep inside her.

And then it happened. The heat of his body behind her. The knowledge that she didn't know this man. A sense of danger that she couldn't control. A shiver ran up her body and breathing became more difficult.

When would this feeling of fear stop? She was safe now. This man clearly wasn't a threat.

Or was he? Those mesmerizing green eyes seemed to see deep inside her and she couldn't help but fear what he might find if he looked too close. And that flutter of attraction that had run through her right before her survival instincts kicked in and took control.

Yeah, this man could most definitely be a threat to the peace she hoped to find here on this tiny island.

As if realizing that they were standing too close, he moved back allowing her to take a deep breath. Squaring her shoulders, she forced her breathing to slow. This was not the first impression she wanted to make on someone who would be one of her new co-workers. *Never show your weaknesses*, her father had always said.

"Sorry, I didn't mean to interrupt you. Yes, I'm Katie McGee. I'm here to set up my orientation." She tried to smile as she turned toward the man, but it was all she could do to keep herself upright. She just needed a couple more minutes for her body to realize it was safe. She'd been through this so often now that she could almost time how long it took for her heart rate to return to normal and her stomach to settle. The fact that she was recovering from these little spells of hers faster than she was only a month ago had to mean that her total recovery was getting closer. Hopefully, a couple of months in more laid-back surroundings than New York City would help her get over this anxiety that came whenever she was in a situation that she didn't feel she could control.

"Oh, sorry," the man said as he grabbed a dish towel, wiped his hands and then held one out. "Dylan. Dylan Maddox. Flight paramedic, assistant manager and, as of four days ago, acting supervisor of the Key West flight crew. Sorry about the smell. I keep forgetting to set the timer."

Katie backed away from the window and looked around the room. She wished Alex had told her more about the man he had left in charge and who would be her boss until he returned. He'd been so rushed the day he'd called and asked for her help that she'd only had time to ask just the most elementary of questions concerning the operation of the local Key West office.

Realizing he still held his hand out to her, she extended her own hand. Warm fingers grasped hers in a firm grip then released.

"It's nice to meet you, Dylan. I still can't believe Alex left the way he did. Is everything okay?" she asked.

"I don't really know. He seemed pretty shook up."

"It's not like him to leave like this. He's always been so dependable." A trait they had in common. But it had been over a year since she had seen him. Maybe the slower pace of the island life had changed him.

"Let's go to the office. He left your paperwork with me." He led her down a short hall off the kitchen, giving her a tour of the building as they walked.

"We have four bedrooms. They're small, but no one has to share," he said as they passed several closed doors, "There are two Jack-and-Jill bathrooms between the rooms. And of course you've already seen the kitchen and our lounge."

He opened the door at the end of the hall where a small desk sat with a tall bookcase behind it. "Alex wanted me to tell you how much he appreciated you coming to help. With me taking over some of the office responsibilities and other members of the crews taking summer vacations we need the extra help."

"He's always been a good friend to me. Besides, I'm getting eight weeks in sunny Florida. My New York flight crew was jealous that I was offered the assignment." And it couldn't have come at a better time. With her family pressuring her to get back to living her life, this job gave her the distance she needed right now. "I just wish I knew he was okay."

Alex's only family as far as she knew was his mother, a well-known Broadway actress, but that wasn't something that he shared with many people. She felt sure she would have heard something if his mother was ill. With her popularity as an actress on the Broadway circuit, the media would quickly have a story out if something had happened to her.

"He didn't really share what the emergency was, but he did say he'd call when he could. And he left all the information you would need with me," Dylan said as he started going through a file on his desk. "It looks like all the paperwork for your Florida nursing license is here along with all your education requirements. I see you've got quite a collection of certifications here too."

"I take my job and my qualifications very seriously," she said. She'd go head-to-head with any of the crew here as far as skills were concerned.

"I can see that," he said as he leaned back in the chair across from her.

She felt like a small ant under a microscope while he studied her. She started to make a comment, but decided she wasn't in the position to get on the wrong side of the man who would be in charge of her till Alex returned. What was it about this man that rattled her so?

She took a moment to study the man herself. He was of average height, but his muscular built was anything but average. His light brown hair was interwoven with blond highlights that no doubt came from time spent in the Florida sun. The man could have made a million bucks as a model in New York. Not that she'd tell him that. Men with looks like his got more attention than was good for them already. She knew that from her own experience. She'd grown up with four very handsome brothers.

She straightened in the chair when he got up and closed the door behind her.

"Look, Katie," he said, sitting back down in his chair, "I'm going to be honest with you. When Alex spoke to me about bringing someone new down here, I had my misgivings. Our flight team is very tight. We work well together because we've been doing it so long. I know each one of the crew's strengths and weaknesses, and they know mine. We have each other's backs every time we go out on a flight together. Not knowing how someone is going to handle themselves out there can put us all at risk."

Was this supposed to be the welcoming speech? Because so far, she was feeling everything but welcomed. Instead, she was thinking that maybe she needed to load back into her brother's old Jeep that she'd borrowed for the trip and head back up north. But she wouldn't. She needed this time alone to get herself together. Just a little bit of time to deal with what she'd been through in the last few months. Her jaw tightened and her chin tipped up. McGees didn't run home when things got tough. McGees stayed till the job was done.

"But looking at this folder, I understand why Alex wanted you here. And it shows how much your friends mean to you that you'd leave your home to come all the way down here to help Alex out. I think that's something we can work with," Dylan said as he leaned back in the chair again.

"Alex told you about the shooting?" she asked. It wasn't as if the incident in New York hadn't made the national news. There had to be cable news stations even this far into the swamps.

"He did. He was very happy that you recovered so quickly. Something like what happened to you can change a person for life," he said.

"And the rest of the team? Do they know?" she asked. She knew as the new kid on the crew there'd be a lot of curiosity about her even if they didn't know about the shooting.

"If they do, they didn't hear it from me. I do know that they'll be happy to have some extra help. We help cover our second local office in Marathon and their staff covers ours when needed."

"I'm happy to be of use wherever you need me. I can start tomorrow," she said, hoping she didn't sound as anxious as she felt. Work had become her security blanket. It was something she was good at. It felt normal, right, when everything else felt off.

An alarm, long and shrill, sounded on a phone. Standing, he pulled his phone from his belt. She heard the doors open down the hall before he opened the door.

"Be safe," Dylan called as she watched the back of three dark blue flight suits rush down the hall.

"Always," one of the crew shouted back at him.

"What's the flight?" she asked as she joined Dylan in the doorway, her heart beating wildly with the adrenaline from the sound of the dispatcher she could hear over the crew's radios as they headed off.

"Pedestrian versus scooter in the historical district. It's too tight an area to land in, but the EMTs called it out as a head injury so we'll meet them at the airport and fly the patient into Miami where there's a neurosurgeon available."

She'd done some studying of the area's available health care before she'd started the trip down and had learned that some specialties weren't provided by the local hospital, which was why it was so important for a helicopter crew to be available in the Keys.

"Like I was saying, I can start tomorrow," she said.

The phone rang on the desk and he walked back over to answer it then put the caller on hold before handing her a large envelope on the table. "Let's discuss when you start after you get settled. The code to the keypad of your rental and a map to its location are in here. I'll get in contact with you later today and we'll set up your orientation then."

He picked up his phone and punched something into it. Her phone immediately dinged and she pulled it out of her pocket.

"My number in case you need to get lost or need anything," Dylan said.

"Thanks." She stood.

She took the envelope, then left the office and found her way back to the front entrance. The humidity that had greeted her the moment she'd driven into Miami enveloped her as she stepped outside and she remembered the promise she'd made to herself of a long shower the minute she got settled into her new place. She took out the map and studied it, surprised to find that it had been hand drawn in bright colored crayons with illustrations that appeared to be fancy stick people and squares that represented buildings. Fortunately, someone had written over the roads in ink with street names and numbers and had also labeled some of the buildings. But it was the words written in bright red crayons that made her smile. Welcome to Key West was printed in large letters across the top of the paper. Not wanting to take any chances, though, she entered the address into her phone. She'd have to ask Alex when he returned for the name of the artist responsible for such a unique map. She just hoped he didn't say it was him.

"Is she nice?" Violet asked as they climbed the steps to the little cottage that was rented out to Katie.

"She seems very nice, but that doesn't mean you can ask her a bunch of questions. She's had a long trip to get here from New York, so she's probably too tired to feel like talking right now. How about we give her a few days to settle in before you give her the Violet inquisition?" Dylan said as he adjusted the basket of fruit and cheese in his arms so that he could hug his daughter to his side.

It amazed him to think of this perfect little eight-year-old as his. Not having known about her until a year ago, he was still new to fatherhood. Some days were harder than others, but they were making it work. His only fear was that her mother would show up one day and undo everything he'd done to make Violet feel like she had a stable home here with him. The idea of her mother taking her back out on the road with her, never knowing exactly where his daughter was… that was something that he couldn't let himself dwell on.

"How many are a few? Two?" she asked.

"Honey, if you make it to two days without driving this poor woman crazy with your questions, it will be a miracle." The door opened and the woman they'd been discussing stood in front of him. Her dark blond hair was down now and it fell past her shoulders and she was wearing an old Mets T-shirt and a pair of torn shorts. She looked much different from the every-hair-perfectly-in-place woman he had met earlier that day. Now she was a woman he could picture himself spending time with.

And where had that thought come from? He didn't have time or any interest in spending time with anyone besides his daughter.

"Ah, hello," Katie said as she blinked her eyes against the sunlight.

Her hair was a bit mussed up and her feet were bare. Did they wake her up from a nap? He should have taken his own advice and let her settle in before he came over, but he was worried he'd been rude this morning.

He wanted to make sure she felt welcome in the community. Even if she was only here temporarily.

What Alex had somehow forgotten to mention was that the big-city girl from New York was also a looker. And right then it was taking all his concentration and the fact that his daughter stood beside him to keep his eyes from a pair of long legs that brought out a very unwanted reaction from him.

"Sorry, we should have waited until tomorrow, but Violet wanted to meet you." He smiled down at the little girl, who was studying the newcomer seriously. "We won't disturb you. I'll just give you this—" he pushed the basket he'd bought at the grocery store into her arms "—and now we'll let you get back to it. I mean get back to resting or whatever."

As he tripped over the words coming out of his mouth, he tried to understand what was happening to him. Yes, this woman with her sleepy emerald bedroom eyes was damn sexy right then, but he didn't even know her. She was a temporary coworker. That was all she could be.

Setting down the basket, she bent down to

his daughter and held out her hand. "Hello, Violet. My name is Katie. I'm so glad to meet you."

"I'm glad to meet you too, but I'm not allowed to ask you any questions for at least two days," his daughter said with a smile that could charm even the most hardened heart.

"Really? And why is that?" Katie asked.

"My daddy says you've had a long trip and are too tired. Are you too tired?" Violet asked, the determined glint in her eyes telling him that there would be no stopping his daughter now.

Katie looked up at him and smiled before turning back to Violet. "I think I could handle a few questions. Would you like to come in?"

"Can we, Daddy?" Violet asked, her eyes begging him to let her have her way. If she ever realized just how hard it was for him to say no to her he'd be in big trouble.

"Are you sure?" he asked. They did need to discuss a few things before the next day.

"Of course. I've still got a few bags to unpack, but most everything is out of the way." She bent to pick the basket up, but he beat her to it.

"I've got this. Do you like the place?" he asked. It would be a little awkward if she started complaining about the cottage.

"I love it! When Alex said he had the perfect place for me to stay, I didn't expect anything like this," she said as they headed inside. For someone who had been half-asleep just seconds before, her face was now animated with a pleasure that for some inexplicable reason pleased him to no end. "You need to see the view in the back. And there's a path that leads down to the water. It's amazing."

Violet giggled from behind the two of them as Katie led them to the large sliding doors at the back of the cottage.

"We think it's the perfect view too," he said. Turning back to his daughter, he winked.

"You do?" Katie asked as she faced them. "You've been here before?"

"My friend Janna lived here for a few weeks, but she had to go home with her parents," Violet said, her tone leaving no room for doubt that she was not happy with her friend's parents.

"Oh, is that how Alex heard about the property?" Katie asked Dylan.

"Sort of. He asked me about a rental and I told him this place was open. I've only had it on the rental market for a couple months."

"You've only had it on the rental market for a couple months?" Katie said, repeating his words. "You own the cottage? You're my landlord?"

"Yes. I assumed Alex would have mentioned my name and the fact that I owned the rental." But there seemed to be a lot that Alex had forgotten to mention. Like how long it would be before he would return and let Dylan get back to his own responsibilities.

"And we're neighbors too," Violet said as she pushed past her father. "Come see."

Violet walked over to the sliding doors and slid one open. "That's our place next door. Isn't it pretty?"

They walked out to the small deck that he had built onto the back of the cottage, so that Katie could see the slightly larger cottage only a few yards away.

"It is very pretty. I love that color of green," Katie said before looking over at him. "You didn't think you should tell me this morning that we would be living next door or that you were my new landlord?"

"I really did think that Alex had told you. It's not like him to forget something like that." Which had him wondering even more what exactly was going on in Alex's life?

"Dylan… I mean Daddy…let me help with all the colors," Violet said. "And he bought me my own tool belt just like his…but it's pink. Do you like pink?"

"I do like pink," Katie told his daughter before turning back to him. "Did you build this yourself?"

"We both did," Violet answered before he could speak. "It's our investment property. Daddy says we need it so that we can pay for our house before he's gray and wrinkled."

"Violet, why don't you run down to the water and see if there are any shells for Katie? I bet she'd like to collect a few to take back to New York," Dylan said. He waited until his daughter was out of earshot before continuing their conversation. "Sorry, she gets a little excited when she meets new people."

"She's adorable. I just wish I had some of her energy," Katie said. She pushed her hair away from her face, but the soft gulf breeze blew it right back. "Would you like some water? I'm afraid that's all I have right now. I should have stopped at the store on the way here, but I was so tired of driving. I don't think I, or the Jeep, could have gone any further."

"No, we're good," he said. "I was surprised when Alex said you were driving down. That's a trip not too many people would be willing to make."

"It seemed like a good time for a road trip. You know, get some fresh air. Clear the mind. I am glad, though, that I don't have to think about that return trip for a few weeks. I was surprised with how tired you can get just sitting in a seat for twelve hours."

"I'm sorry we got interrupted this morning. And I admit even though I thought Alex had mentioned my owning the cottage, I should have discussed it with you this morning." He'd known the minute he'd gotten off the phone call from the regional office that he should have made some comment about being her landlord instead of just throwing a map and key code at her as she walked out the door.

He had a lot to learn about being a landlord.

"It was a little crazy this morning. How

did the flight go?" she asked, taking a seat on one of the wicker chairs he'd purchased for the deck. It was strange seeing this big-city woman in an old ratty shirt and shorts appearing so at home on the deck of his little cottage. He'd only known her for a day, even less, but something about her intrigued him.

Or was it just his need to take care of everyone? He'd learned from Alex and her employee file that Katie had been through some difficult times and he knew they weren't over yet. No one went through what she had without coming out scarred.

And he couldn't help but think that the last time a woman had interested him this much, it hadn't ended well. Except for Violet. Violet made all the heartache her mother had caused him worth it.

"He had an open-head injury, but the prognosis was good when the crew dropped him off at the Miami trauma unit. We'll check back with the hospital tomorrow and see how he's doing," he said as he took a matching chair across from her.

"Do you get many of those? Pedestrian versus vehicles injuries? Most everyone I saw on my way to the cottage was on a bike or walking in this area."

"There are more than a few tourists that decide getting on a bicycle after drinking or driving a scooter when they haven't been on one for years is a good idea. Fortunately, most only end up with skinned knees or broken arms that can be treated in the local hospital. But there are enough of the serious injuries to keep us busy flying back and forth to the mainland. Of course, we have our share of boating accidents and drownings too."

"It sounds much different from what I'm use to in New York," Katie said. She was looking into the thin line of trees that separated the cottage from the water, but he could tell her mind was somewhere else. Was it back to the night of the shooting? Alex had told him enough about the incident that he knew she'd required several weeks in the hospital.

"About what I said this morning, about me having doubts about you coming here at first, I don't want you to think we aren't glad to have you. You will find that our small crew works well together and I have no doubts that they'll be happy you are here to help. And with Alex speaking so highly of you, I do think this is a good place for you." Hearing his daughter coming up the path, he stood to go.

"I understand. The New York office was concerned about me coming back after the shooting, but I proved myself to them."

"I know. Alex told me they were impressed." He didn't tell her that Alex himself had mentioned some concerns after talking to her, though his boss hadn't been able to pinpoint what was wrong. "How about we start with your orientation tomorrow morning?"

"Look what I found for you, Katie," Violet said as she climbed the step up to the deck as she held out two shells for Katie to examine.

"They're very pretty. I'll have to get something to keep them in so I can take them back to New York with me." Katie took the shells from his daughter.

"We have a bunch at our house if you want to come see them," his daughter offered.

"Why don't we let her get settled first," Dylan said as they walked back through the cottage to the front door.

"But..." Violet started to protest.

"What have I told you about our neighbors?" Dylan asked his daughter, brushing his hand over her curls. It was the only thing she'd gotten from him. Her slim build and baby blue eyes were a replica of her mother.

"They're not here for our entertainment. We have to respect their privacy." Violet repeated to him in a sad singsong voice.

"What time do you want me at the office?" Katie asked as they reached the door.

"Shift change is seven. If there isn't a call we'll take a ride over the islands so you can get your bearings. Then we'll get your schedule set up."

"Sounds great. I'll see you then. And, Violet," she said, calling out to his daughter who was skipping up and down the sidewalk, "maybe you can come back to help me gather some shells another day?"

His daughter jumped with joy and he listened all the way home to the description of all the shells that she hoped to collect for her new friend, Katie.

CHAPTER TWO

THEY LIFTED OFF the ground and as the helicopter skids rose, so did Katie's spirit. She'd missed this when she'd been injured and unable to fly. She'd missed all of it. The tight quarters, the equipment bags, the speed as they climbed higher and then shot through the air. There had been no way for her to accept that her job as a flight nurse was over. This was as much a part of her life as breathing. It wasn't just what she did. It was who she was. It was why she had worked so hard to get back in the air as fast as possible.

Then she looked down and caught her breath. While Key West was larger than she had first assumed, from the air, with its small landmass surrounded by an unending view of blue water, it was like looking down on a small neighborhood in New York City. And the trees. Everywhere she looked there were colorful flowering trees that based on their size had to be hundreds of years old. That was something she didn't see much of in the city.

"Roy, can you take us south and then north up Highway One?" Dylan said over the headset.

"That's the highway I came in on. The only way in or out, right?" she said, speaking into the headset.

"It's the only road access, but we have a lot of boat traffic. We get called out for boating accident victims a few times a month. We also have a port where the cruise ships stop." He pointed over to where a large ship sat. "Occasionally there's a passenger that needs to be flown out to Miami, but most of the time their passengers end up in the local hospital for minor problems. Most of what we see is traumas or transfers from the hospital to a higher level of care."

"And this is what is known as the southernmost tip of the island," Roy said as they passed over a small area of rocks and water before they turned and headed north.

They quickly crossed the rest of the island

and were following the path of the highway that would take them all the way up the coast and back to the mainland when both Dylan's and Roy's radios went off. She listened as the county dispatcher gave out coordinates of a motor vehicle crashand the channel on their radio where they would receive info on their landing location.

"Ten-four. We're in the air and responding to call. ETA under five minutes," Roy answered back to the dispatcher as they continued heading north.

"We're taking the call?" Katie said as she opened a drawer labeled IV Supplies and began to prepare a bag of fluids. Fortunately, all the Heli-Care copters were stocked the same, with their drawers labeled for quick access. "I thought this was an orientation flight."

"The Marathon crew the dispatcher was talking about is our sister crew. They're already on the scene and have requested backup. There must be more than two injured needing to be flown out to Miami. You said you were ready. Is there a problem?" Dylan said as he began checking their bags for supplies that could be needed if an intubation was required.

"No, of course not," she said as the adrenaline began to pump through her. If only she didn't feel like an trainee that was about to perform for their preceptor. She'd done these calls hundreds of times. Why was she second-guessing herself? This was just what she was wanting a few minutes ago.

"Switching to channel three for landing zone instructions," Roy said.

She listened over the headphones as Roy contacted the local fire department, which had secured the landing zone on the highway. As they got closer, she could see where traffic was backed up for at least a mile headed both north and south. Bringing traffic to a standstill on the only road in and out of the islands had to put more pressure on the first responders.

"This is Heli-Care Key West awaiting instructions for landing," Roy announced over the radio.

She saw another helicopter lift off into the sky and head north, freeing up the area for their own landing.

As the helicopter lifted, a voice came over

the channel "This is local Conch Key fire and rescue. Is that you, Roy?"

"Yeah, Jones. What's happening down there? All we got from dispatch was MVC. Is the landing zone secured?" Roy asked.

"Zone secured, but it's a mess down here. Camper jackknifed into oncoming lane. Driver and passenger of second vehicle are headed to Miami for trauma. They're working on a passenger in the vehicle pulling the camper right now," the firefighter said. "The sooner you get down here the better."

Katie's stomach clinched as they started into their final approach. She forced herself to take a deep breath, and then glanced over to see that Dylan was watching her. "I'm fine. Just a few nerves. New place and everything."

Her confidence might have taken a beating, but except for a few bruises she was fit and ready to work. She just had to remind herself of that sometimes.

The skids touched down, and the two of them quickly unloaded their stretcher and scene bag as they stayed below the rotors.

Following the man she assumed was Jones, they hurried toward the scene. What was once a small travel trailer was now in pieces scattered across the middle of the road with a small compact car crushed beside it. There was no doubt that the driver and any passengers in the vehicle would be in critical condition.

Crossing a small medium, she saw a pickup truck on its side against a tree with several firefighters surrounding it. An ambulance crew was stationed beside the truck, but it was easy to see that their patient was still trapped inside the vehicle.

"What's the holdup?" Dylan asked as they approached the EMTs.

"The door crushed in on impact and they needed to use their rescue equipment on the victims in the car first. They were both unresponsive on arrival. They said this guy was talking when they arrived."

She followed Dylan as he moved to where the first responders worked. From the language of the firefighters that were operating the Jaws of Life, things weren't going well.

"How's our patient?" he asked as he moved to look inside the crushed front end of the truck. "You couldn't get him out through the window?"

"The way the top folded in on it, it was faster to go in this way," a man closest to the wrecked truck said. "When the trailer jack-knifed, it hit the side rail before hitting the tree. The whole truck was crushed."

"We're in," a firefighter said, and then moved back as Dylan moved to the opening.

Leaving the stretcher, Katie grabbed their bag. An older man, she estimated to be in his fifties, was still attached by his seat belt in the driver's seat.

"I thought they said he was talking," she said, opening their scene bag and pulling out a collar to secure the man's neck.

"He was until about two minutes ago," a fireman said as he joined them.

"Can you bring the backboard and stretcher over here," she asked the him as she watched Dylan check the man's pulse.

"He's got a pulse, but his respiration is shallow. He needs intubating but there's no way to do it without moving him first. Let's get him out and secured." Dylan took the cervical collar from her and secured it before moving back to let the firefighters transfer him to the stretcher.

She grabbed an endotracheal tube and laryngoscope and readied them for intubation. Handing them off to Dylan as soon as the man had been strapped to the backboard, she pulled out an IV kit and started working on getting access. Going for a big bore site, she cleaned the man's antecubital vein. As she inserted the needle, she suddenly became aware of a group of men crowding her back.

A bunch of nosy first responders was the last thing she needed to deal with right now.

She flushed the line and hung the bag of fluid she'd prepared earlier. Turning around, she gave the crowd of firefighters and EMTs a look that would have had her older brothers shaking in their NYPD-issued boots. Of course this group of adrenaline junkies didn't have the good sense to give her some space.

"Problem?" Dylan asked as he slid the tube into their patient's trachea.

"No. I've got this," she said as she applied the patches and hooked the man to the portable monitor. His heart rate was elevated, in the one-twenties. The men behind her pressed in even closer.

"The whole bunch of you need to take a step back." When they didn't move, she raised her voice. *"Now."*

As she turned back to her patient, she heard some of the men laugh while others complained. As she and Dylan began to rush their patient back to the helicopter, she overheard one of the men say that she must be a rookie.

They'd been on-site just over ten minutes and part of that time had been waiting for their patient to be cleared from the wreckage. The two of them had worked together as if they had for years. There was no one she had ever worked with that could have done things any better.

"Ignore them," Dylan said as she climbed into the helicopter. "They're just curious about a newcomer. It's one of the problems with living on a small island. It won't last long."

"I handled it," she said, then put the comments she'd heard behind her. There were more important things here than whether a bunch of first responders liked her. She wasn't there to be liked. She was there to keep this guy alive till they could hand him off to the closest trauma unit.

She had begun her assessment before the skids even left the ground, calling out her findings to Dylan as he radioed report to the receiving hospital in Miami.

"I'm only getting breath sounds on the right side and his oxygen sats are in the mideighties," she told him after he signed off the radio.

"Pneumo?" Dylan asked. "Or tube placement?"

Was this a test? With the extent of the man's injuries it could easily be a pneumothorax, but without an X-ray to verify placement or determine if there was a pneumo, the first thing she would normally do was replace the tube. Of course, telling her boss that his tube might not be correctly placed could be awkward, but if they were going to work together they would need honesty. That was something her father had drilled into all his children. If you couldn't trust your partner, who could you trust?

"My instincts say it's a pneumo, but we have another thirty minutes of flight time so we should replace the tube first," she said.

"Should?" he asked. One eyebrow rose above those amazing eyes that were bearing down on her.

"I'm going to replace the endotracheal

tube in case there's a problem with placement," she said with more confidence than she felt. If she'd been back on her own home turf she would have told her partner what she was about to do and unless they'd had any objections she'd have moved on.

Not waiting for Dylan's consent, she pulled out the proper ET tube and supplies. After removing the tube placed by Dylan, she placed the new tube in seconds. Checking placement with her stethoscope she listened to both sides of the man's chest. She shook her head. "Still no sound on the left side."

"His sats are still holding in the high eighties and his blood pressure is stable right now. I think we can hold off and let the trauma center put in the chest tube. You agree?" Dylan asked.

"I do. The best thing for this guy is to get him to a surgeon. He's holding his pressure right now, but his stomach's tight. He's bleeding somewhere internally," she said as she was adjusting the IV fluids to give the patient a bolus to help replace the blood she knew he was losing. She reached into the man's pants pocket, checking one and then the other and finally locating a billfold. She handed it to Dylan. "The hospital will want this. His phone must still be in the truck. Maybe one of the officers will find it and can notify his family."

"Fifteen-minute ETA," Roy said over the headphones. "Heli-Care Marathon should be cleared out by the time we arrive. Then it's back home for us, right, boss? I think Katie's pretty much got a good lay of the land by now, don't you?"

"Ten-four, Roy. I think we can head home as soon as we unload. Time to get back to the surf and sand." Dylan turned toward her with a smile that sent her heartbeat racing. This man could be a real charmer when he wanted to be.

"Whatever you say, boss," she said as she smiled back, "whatever you say."

"How did the newbie do, boss? I heard you got dispatched together." Katie heard a male voice ask. Stopping before she entered the office, she tried to remember if this was one of the two men she'd met that morning. Feeling self-conscious, and a little bit curious, she waited to hear Dylan's answer.

"She's not a newbie; she has as many years

as you do in flying. And stop calling me 'boss.'"

Okay, he hadn't sung her praises, but he had let the man know she was an experienced flight nurse.

"I heard she let the guys shake her up like a newbie," the man, who was really starting to get on her nerves said. What was his name? Casey? No, that was the flight nurse going off shift.

"You know we need someone we can count on, not some big-city nurse who doesn't understand how we do things around here," the man continued.

"I heard she had a bad scene in New York and took a bullet for her patient," a female voice said, "that sounds like someone you can count on to me."

If she wasn't mistaken it was Summer's voice that she heard defending her now. It had to be since she was the only woman on the shift till tomorrow morning. She'd known she was going to like the petite blonde the moment she'd met her. Though, she did wish everyone didn't know the story of her being injured at a scene. It seemed nothing traveled faster than a juicy story. Or maybe Alex told

Summer before he'd left? She'd asked Katie several questions that morning about where Alex could have taken off to. As if Katie had any more information than the rest of them. If anyone was to know where Alex was, it should have been Dylan.

Alex had always been so vague about his family. It couldn't have been easy having the paparazzi hounding him and his mother when he was growing up. And he'd never mentioned anything about his father.

"I also heard she choked the first time she went out on a flight in New York after the shooting," the man answered Summer back. "That's not cool. You know we all rely on each other here. I'm sure we're just a bunch of beach bums to her, but we can't go around insulting our firefighters and EMTs without ruffling some feathers. We depend on those guys for our safety."

"It seems to me you've all been spending too much time listening to gossip that doesn't have anything to do with you or your job. I hear what you're saying, Max. I don't know exactly what happened when she went back to work, but I can assure you she was fully cleared to work before she left New York and she did a great job on the scene today. I'd be happy to fly with her anytime. And yes, Katie's new here so maybe the guys at the scene should have given her some room."

As the door started to swing open, Katie turned and rushed toward the kitchen. The only thing that would be more embarrassing than overhearing her coworkers' objections to her working there would be for her to get caught.

An older man came into the kitchen and gave her a weak smile before heading off to the lounge where she heard the television volume increase. When Summer didn't follow him, Katie figured she'd gone to her quarters to rest.

The smart thing to do was to just pretend that she hadn't heard the conversation, but was that really the right thing to do? If she was already having problems with the staff not trusting her, what future did she have here?

But that was just her lack of confidence talking. Alex said himself that he'd be willing to fly with her. She couldn't ask for anything more than that as his vote of confidence in her.

All she had ever wanted to be was a flight nurse since the first time she'd seen a helicopter take off of the roof on the hospital where she had first started as a new nurse. She'd made that her focus for three years, taking classes and getting certifications and experience in the intensive care units so she could meet the necessary qualifications. Her father had bragged to all his buddies on the police force that his daughter was now flying the skies of New York saving lives. She'd used her father's pride in her as motivation at rehab so she could get back the physical stamina she needed to return to work.

Alex knew all this about her. He knew that she would never let anything stand in the way of her doing her job. But Dylan? He didn't know her at all.

"Hey," Dylan said, startling her as he stepped into the kitchen, "I thought you were going to come finish your paperwork."

"Sorry, I just stopped to get a bottle of water." She held up the bottle before following him back to the office.

"How much did you hear?" he asked as he shut the door behind them.

She should have known Dylan was an everything-up-front kind of guy. He had known she was headed to the office right behind the two flight crew members and while he could have pretended that she hadn't overheard them, he wasn't going to do it.

"Enough," she said. Enough to know she was already starting off on the wrong foot. He'd told her that this was a good crew that worked closely together. Her plan had been to keep her head down and work hard for the next two months, but on her first flight she'd managed to bring too much unwanted attention to herself.

"You want to talk about it?" he asked as he leaned back on the corner of the desk.

"Not really," she replied. What could she say? That all of this was because of the simple fact she couldn't handle that feeling of defenselessness she felt whenever someone came up behind her? Didn't that just sound like a strong, capable nurse you would want on your team?

"And why is that, Katie? Afraid someone might see a kink in that armor you're wearing? We've all got our issues. Take Max. He can't handle a puking patient so he carries an emesis bag with him at all times. It's how he handles it." His eyes searched hers.

Was it possible that this man could see the fear she barely kept hidden? Would he see how broken she was? She'd been able to keep her anxiety to herself, even hiding it from her family of hard-core police officers. How could this man see inside her so easily? She'd thought she was safe because Alex wasn't there. It seemed she was wrong. Dylan saw too much.

"Look, I've been through a lot the last few months, but one thing I know for sure is that nothing that happened has affected my caring for my patients." Like her father had told her when she'd come out of surgery, she couldn't lie in bed feeling sorry for herself. If she wanted to show the coward that had shot her that he hadn't won, she had to get up and get back to work.

And that was what she had done. Only it hadn't been as easy as her father had made it sound. She'd healed on the outside, but there was still something on the inside that wasn't ready to move on. But that wasn't something she was going to admit to Dylan.

"Alex told me everything he knew about

your injuries. I know you were shot by some punk who didn't care who he hurt while he was trying to finish off his first victim. I know you placed yourself in front of your patient and took a bullet. I know that your patient died with you lying injured over him. And while Alex seemed to think that you were back a hundred percent, I find that a little hard to believe," Dylan said, his eyes still locked with hers.

"What do you mean? I've done everything my doctors have asked. I worked my butt off in rehab." She broke contact with him, afraid to see the pity she'd seen so much of when her coworkers had come to visit her in the hospital.

"I'm not questioning that you're up to the job here. I have no complaints about your performance today." He ran his hands through the curls that were working their way down into his eyes. "Look, Katie, I know it's hard to admit that you need help. It's hard for everyone. I just want you to know that if you want to talk to someone I'm here."

"What, like you want to be my new counselor? You have to know I've already gone through all the counseling sessions that are required after a traumatic injury. It has to be there in my employment record somewhere." The vulnerability from having this stranger know so much about her made her want to strike out. What did he really know? What did anyone know about her life now?

"Have you ever had to do it? Sat down in some office and bare all your personal feelings and failings?" she asked, knowing what his answer would be. There was no way this tough guy would ever admit that he had some type of weakness.

"Yes, actually I have. It was only once, but after a particularly bad scene when I was first starting off I was having problems sleeping. I have a friend who went into psychology who has an office in Islamorada so I went to talk to him," Dylan said as he leaned back in his chair.

"Did it help?" she asked, "Did it make any difference?"

"I can't say it was an instant fix-all, but it felt like just admitting to someone and sharing that I was having a problem with what I had seen, and having him say that it was okay, even expected, for me to have the reaction I was having helped. Soon after that, we started doing debriefing after our flights. I think that's helped us all."

"But that's different. Your friend wasn't in a position to decide if you were able to work or not. Your future wasn't being determined by him." And that didn't sound a bit paranoid, did it?

"I'm just saying if you need someone to talk to, I'm here for you just as I'd be there for any of the crew. Or I could see about getting you set up with my friend here if you think that would work better for you. He's a good man." Dylan stood and handed her a folder. "Here's the paperwork that you need to finish. You can bring it by the cottage if you want. I'll email you a copy of the schedule I'm reworking before I leave today."

"Thanks," she said as she took the folder and turned to leave. She knew she should say more. He was only trying to do his job. She should be grateful that he cared about her. After all, she was only there for the next two months. All he really had to care about was whether she showed up for her shifts or not. But that didn't make it any easier to take.

"And, Katie," Dylan said from behind her, "don't worry about Max. He can be a little grumpy, but put him out on a scene and he'll have your back."

She turned around and met Dylan's eyes as he added, "We'll *all* have your back."

CHAPTER THREE

KATIE'S PHONE RANG as soon as she opened the door to her cottage. After her talk with Dylan, she was sure it was her counselor calling again. The woman was a nice person. It wasn't her fault that she had been assigned to Katie's case, which required her to check on her once a month. If only the woman didn't ask so many questions.

Seeing that instead it was her younger brother, she answered the call. "Hey, Mikey."

"Sis, why haven't you called anyone? Matt's been going crazy wondering if his Jeep is okay," her brother said.

"I'm glad to hear that it wasn't me he was worried about," she teased. Laying down the folder of paperwork she had to fill out onto the small dining table, she moved over to the French doors and opened the curtains. Paradise was just outside her back door. It was the perfect place for her to escape her worries.

"You know that all of us worry about you, especially now that you're over fourteen hundred miles away. You sure you don't want to come home?" Her brother had been asking the same question every day since she left New York.

She knew that her brothers loved her and she could always count on them to have her back. If only they understood she needed a little space right now.

"Katie, did you hear me? Is everything okay?" her brother asked.

"Sorry. I just got home from the office and my mind is kind of scattered," she said. After grabbing a bottle of water from the fridge, she unlocked the back door.

"How did it go? Did you get to see your friend Alex?" Mikey asked.

"No, he's still out of town on some type of family emergency. But I did get to go up today," she said. Stepping out onto the deck, she took a deep breath. The air was heavy with a humidity she didn't think she could ever get used to, but the soft breeze coming from the water made up for it.

"How was that?" he asked. "Any issues?"

If she told her little brother about almost losing her temper with the other emergency responders, he'd know something was wrong. McGees were known for their patience, and normally she was the most patient of the siblings. With four brothers, she had to be.

"No, it was great. I wish you could see this place. It's beautiful. The water is so blue and everywhere you look there's some tree or bush blooming. And the pace seems so much slower here."

Something moved in the short bushes that backed up to the deck. She eased back toward the French door even though her mind told her she was safe. A large yellow beak peaked out of a bush before it disappeared through the trees. A bird? She took the stairs down from the deck and followed the sandy path that Violet had used to get to the water.

"That's good, right? Not that I want you to get used to it. We still need you here in New York," her brother said. "What about that counselor from the precinct? You still talking with her?"

Hadn't she already dealt with this enough today? No one understood how hard it was to bare your soul to a stranger who clearly did not understand that all she needed was to work and put the shooting behind her. She wasn't going to let this one incident define her life.

She stopped on the path, not daring to even breathe. A large white bird stood a mere five feet in front of her. Its dark legs, long and spindly, made it over three feet tall. Was it dangerous? Would it follow her if she ran back into the house?

Before she could decide what to do, it unfolded a pair of impossibly large wings, making its size even more intimidating. With a couple flaps it soared into the sky, leaving her standing there with her mouth open. She stood and watched as its magnificent wings took it out of sight.

The sound of her brother's voice brought her back down to reality.

"Oh, my goodness, Mikey. There was this bird. This really big bird…like three-foot-tall big. It was beautiful. So beautiful. It was white and…" She stopped talking, suddenly hit with a need she hadn't felt since…since before her life had been shattered into a million meaningless pieces.

"I've got to go. I'll call you later," she said as she ended the call and raced up the path to the cottage as fast as she could. She tried to keep the image in her mind.

She found her sketch pad and pencils in an unpacked box stuck in the back of the closet. Rushing back outside, she sat on a wicker chair and pulled a small table in front her where she could arrange her supplies, and then she began. In minutes the image of a beautiful, but strong bird began to take shape. As the light began to fade with the setting sun in front of her, she filled in the background with the many different shrubs and flowering trees that she was just beginning to notice. She'd have to ask Dylan the names of all these plants. Maybe she could buy one of the smaller ones to bring back home with her.

Finally setting her sketch pad down, she realized how much she had enjoyed the last few hours. She couldn't remember the last time she'd truly relaxed for that long. It was like she had found her happy place, even if it would be for only a few weeks. She was right. All she needed was a little peace and quiet, and soon her life would be back to normal.

She headed inside and saw the folder she had meant to get back to Dylan. Before putting her art supplies away, she sat down and finished the paperwork. A peek in the mirror told her she needed to do something with her hair as the breeze had made a mess of it. She pulled it back into a careless knot then washed her face.

Checking her phone, she wasn't surprised to see that she'd missed a call from her brother. He must think she was crazy for hanging up on him like she had. She'd take a picture of her drawing and send it to him before she went to bed. He'd understand then. He'd always been the only one in the family that understood how much her art meant to her.

It was only after she rang the doorbell of Dylan's cottage that she realized it was probably too late for her to be visiting her neighbor. Why hadn't she thought to text him? He'd given her his number for things just like this. She started back down the stairs.

Dylan stood in the door staring down at something he'd never seen before: a smiling Katie. She waited on the bottom step of his home and something about that smile made his insides suddenly warm and weak.

"I'm so sorry. I wanted to get the paperwork back to you. I meant to get it to you earlier, but I got busy and I'm afraid I didn't realize how late it was." She held the folder out to him. "I guess I could blame it on the bird, but it really was all my fault."

"A bird? Why do I feel like there's a story there?" he asked. She really wasn't making much sense, but he wanted her to keep talking. There was something different about her tonight. Or maybe not different. Maybe this was the real Katie McGee. The one his friend Alex had told him about that was always smiling and fun. The intense woman he'd been with earlier that day had shown no sign of either of those two things.

"I was just in the backyard and there was this big white bird. It wasn't a stork. I've seen pictures of them before, they're stockier. But it was tall and it had these dark legs and big wings," Katie said.

"It sounds like a great white heron. We have them everywhere. There's a wildlife refuge set up for them here in the Keys. They're very common around here," he explained.

"A white heron? I knew there were blue herons, but not white ones. Aren't they beautiful?" she asked, another smile lighting her face.

"Very, beautiful," he said. Her eyes sparkled with excitement that he saw every day when his eight-year-old made a new discovery. There were so many wonders on the island that he suddenly wanted to show her. So many things that he knew she would find enjoyment in.

Like a gust of wind, his daughter suddenly blew past him and down the steps to where Katie stood.

"Hey, Katie, what's that?" Violet asked.

His mind switched gears and he was reminded that his daughter was his priority. Not spending time with his new neighbor.

"I had a visitor today in the back of the house. Your father says it's a white heron," Katie said, passing Violet her drawing.

"Daddy took me to the park where there's a lot of these up in the trees in their nests. It's where they take care of their babies," Violet said, then handed back the sketch pad. "Maybe next time you can go with us. Can she, Daddy?"

Dylan looked down at the two of them, Violet with her hopeful eyes that had seen way too much for her eight years of life. And Katie, who just hours ago had been determined to prove to everyone that she was fine but anyone that looked at her could see the shadows under her eyes. While the first one held his heart, the latter brought out that old protective side of him that he knew he couldn't acknowledge. Not where Katie was concerned. He'd had enough of women coming into his life and wreaking havoc before leaving him to pick up the pieces.

"We'll see. How about you go jump in the tub? It's getting late. You did say you wanted to ride the bus tomorrow," he reminded her.

"Okay, but can I go over to Katie's when I get home tomorrow?" she asked with puppy dog eyes.

"We'll see," he said. He'd learned early that his daughter was a true negotiator with a talent that had gotten the best of him more than once. And once she got the answer she wanted, there was no way budging her no matter what might have come up. "Katie might have plans."

"Unless I'm working I don't have any plans," Katie said.

"Great. There's a big book in the library at school that has pictures of birds. I'll finish the book I checked out last week before I go to bed and check that one out if it's there. That way I can teach you about all the birds we have here," Violet said.

"There's not going to be any reading time tonight it you don't get in the tub. Now," he told his daughter.

"Night, Katie," Violet called as she rushed back up the stairs and disappeared into the house.

"Sorry. If she gets to be too much just let me know. We've had to have more than a few conversations concerning boundaries since she came to live with me." He smiled at the memory of that first conversation when he'd brought a date to dinner, and before the meal was over his daughter had somehow gotten the woman's whole life story out of her, including some things that had been more than enough to make him realize there wouldn't be a second date.

"I'm sure we'll be fine. I can't wait to see

the book she's talking about," Katie said. "So, not married?"

"No. It's just me and Violet. Her mother and I were never married." He didn't see any reason to add that he hadn't even known he had a daughter until she and her mother had shown up on the houseboat he was living on at the time. "Lilly, that's Violet's mother, is a bit of a free spirit."

"Well, she seems to be a very happy little girl. I can tell you're doing a good job with her," Katie said. "And I've taken enough of your time. I'll check my email for my schedule."

"If you need to take some time to get settled just let me know. Alex leaves the scheduling up to me and with me filling in for him I've done some rearranging."

"I'm sure whenever you've scheduled me will be fine. Like I said, I don't have any plans right now." She started down the path before turning around and calling back, "Good night."

He didn't take his eyes off her until she had gotten to her front door and disappeared inside.

The woman was one big complication in

his life. But there was something about Katie that made him want to peel back all those layers of armor that surrounded her to find out exactly who she was before her life had changed the night she'd been shot. But how deep would he have to go to find that woman? Did she even exist anymore? Or had the trauma she'd survived changed her forever?

And then there was that spark of attraction he'd felt from the first time they'd met, before he'd known who she was. Before he'd known she was just one more person passing through his life.

"I like her," his daughter said as she ducked under his arm where he stood in the doorway staring across at Katie's cottage.

"I think I do too," he said before turning and shutting the door behind them, wishing he could shut out the warning bells telling him this woman could be trouble. No matter how attracted he might be to his next-door neighbor, the last thing he needed was to find himself involved with another woman who was just passing through the islands. He'd had enough of those relationships even before he had learned that he had a daughter. A daughter that needed the stability she didn't get for the first seven years of her life.

But he couldn't deny how easy it would be to forget his past mistakes after seeing the wide-eyed beauty that had just shown up beaming with excitement over a common white bird.

CHAPTER FOUR

KATIE FOLLOWED SUMMER into the hospital ambulance entrance as the other nurse explained the transfer process between the hospitals. They'd been dispatched to fly a patient from the local hospital to a hospital in Miami that could provide further cardiac diagnostic and treatment for his heart arrhythmia. With the man symptomatic as he continued going in and out of supraventricular tachycardia, the doctor in Miami had requested that he be transferred immediately by air.

"We're a small hospital, but you can't beat the care. It's just impossible for us to provide a lot of the specialties that our patients can get in the big-city hospitals," Summer said as they passed through another door that led to a hallway with an elevator.

"And the staff is always good to work

with," the bubbly nurse continued, and not for the first time that day Katie wondered if Dylan had assigned her with Summer because he knew Katie had overheard Summer sticking up for her in his office.

Not that she was going to complain. If he'd put her with Max for her first shift things could have turned into a nightmare. She had enough of those at night. She didn't want to spend her days that way.

"A lot of the flight crew staff pick up days in the ER when they can," Summer continued as the bell on the elevator rang and she pressed the only button for an upper floor. "Does the crew in New York do that?"

"Several of us do. It's a good way to keep our hospital skills up. And it's a nice change, too, from the pack-up and deliver speed that we are used to on flights." And it had been Katie's backup plan if she'd had to give up flying after the shooting.

"I know. And it's nice to talk to your patients sometimes too. Most of our flights are spent with patients that are too sick to talk. And the flights are usually so short that we spend most of our time too busy to get to know them," Summer said.

So Summer was a people person. She could see that and even appreciate it.

Katie had been that way too. But then things had changed. It seemed her whole life had changed because of one night. It wasn't that she didn't like people. She did like most people on a one-to-one basis. But put her in a crowd, like the one she could see in the room they were about to enter, and the stress of being surrounded by so many strangers was just too much.

She had learned to work around her anxiety. No one thought there was something wrong with a nurse if she asked the family to step out for a moment.

Except for that first flight here, trauma scenes hadn't been a problem because everyone was so busy doing their jobs that they didn't get in each other's way.

Summer introduced her to the charge nurse on the cardiac floor before they entered the room where a fiftyish male lay in the bed surrounded by family members.

"Hello, Mr. Marshall. My name is Summer and this is my partner Katie. We're going to be your flight crew today."

After the information had been given to

his family concerning the Miami hospital they would be flying to and their expected arrival time, they were soon back in the air and headed north.

Their pilot today was Jackie, and like Roy she had been military before retiring and taking a civilian job for Heli-Care. Katie relaxed into her old routine as she applied the monitors that would give them the cardiac tracing and vital sign information critical to their patient's care.

"Weather is looking good for us today. ETA in forty," Jackie said over the headset.

"Looks like this is going to be an easy one," Summer said as she pointed to the monitor where it showed the patient in a normal sinus rhythm.

"I'm glad the doctor agreed to order him some Ativan before we left. Fear of flying can send anyone's heart into tachycardia." Katie adjusted the fluids hanging as Summer recorded the vital signs.

"I love flying. Always have. You?" Summer asked.

"There's nothing like it. I mean look at that view," Katie said, looking down at the water that went from pale green in the shallows to a dark blue as the waters deepened. She could see several groups of people decked out in snorkel gear down below. She made a mental note to see about taking one of the boat tours to the reefs while she was there.

"You must have some great views in the city. Especially at night," Summer said.

"We do," Katie agreed, remembering the flight she'd been on the night she was shot. The lights of the city had been breathtaking. She remembered thinking that she'd sketch the scene out when she got back to their quarters. Then later at home, she'd pull out her paints and try to capture that perfect color of the dark night sky with the lights twinkling on and off from all the high-rise buildings, where some people were shutting down for the night, putting their children to bed and preparing for sleep while others still worked to hammer out a living in the local diner or one of the big corporations that made up the city.

But she'd never gotten the chance to record the beauty of that night. Instead she'd experienced the pain and violence that the darkness of the city had hidden from her until it was too late. Until a man had decided that taking her life was just collateral in his plan to kill someone else.

"Do you live in one of those high-rises? Those New York apartments always look so glamorous on television. It must be a big change living in Dylan's cottage. Not that I wouldn't love to live in that cottage. It's adorable."

"Believe me, my apartment is nothing like the ones you see on television. Most of them aren't. You could easily put two of my apartments into the cottage." And that wasn't even considering the space she had on the back deck.

"I bet you miss it, though. The city. I love it here on the island. I've always been a small-town girl. But sometimes I think about what it would be like to disappear into the crowds and live that fast-paced life," Summer mused.

"Well, if you decide you want to make a change, just let me know. I'd be glad to show you around the city and there's always an opening on our crew," Katie said. She checked their patient's vitals again and noted a small four beat of SVT before the man's heart rhythm returned back to the nineties.

"I don't know. I can't imagine the flights you get. I'm afraid I couldn't keep up with the pace. I don't know how you do it. Especially after what happened."

The monitor alarmed and they both saw the six-beat run of SVT, but once again the man's heart rhythm returned back to the nineties.

Katie checked his vital signs again and charted, glad to have something to keep her busy so she didn't have to continue her conversation with Summer. It seemed her new coworker was just as open about things as Katie was normally. But this was different. She didn't talk about what had happened with anyone except for her counselor and she only did that because she hadn't been given a choice.

"Going in for final landing," Jackie announced into the headsets while Summer was on a different radio station calling ahead with report that dispatch would forward to the receiving hospital.

They began preparations to unload their patient as soon as the skids touched down.

Later, Katie steered the conversation toward work as they made their way back to the Keys. Summer had only been a part of the flight crew for two years, but she had a wealth of information concerning the workings of the local hospital and the helicopter services Heli-Care provided for the community.

They were back in time to order a lunch delivery and after eating agreed that though the shift had been a cakewalk up to then, it could change at any time. It was best for them to get some rest then before the night calls began to come in. With a twenty-four-hour shift, you had to take it when you had a chance.

"How'd it go?" Dylan asked as he came out of the office and met them in the hall. "Good flight?"

"No problems," Summer said as she headed into her assigned room for the shift.

"Katie?" he asked. "Any problems?"

"Simple pack-up and deliver flight. Our patient was stable. He probably could have gone by ground." Was he going to question her every time she went out on a flight? "If you're asking if I behaved myself, I can assure you that I did."

"I wasn't worried about you behaving

yourself. I was just making sure that you didn't need anything. It's only your second flight in a new location. I would check on anyone who had just arrived here. Unfortunately, until Alex gets back that's my job," Dylan added, his lips pulled down into a grim line that she hadn't seen on him before. It had to be stressful having to manage the crew by himself.

And here she was giving him grief because the only thing she had been concentrating on since she got here was herself. She hadn't thought about how much Alex's unexpected leave had burdened Dylan. As a single dad he had a lot of demands on him already, she didn't need to make things harder for him.

"I apologize. I know you're just doing your job. It's just hard feeling like I'm starting over with someone constantly checking on me after being a flight nurse for almost six years." She started opening the door to her room and his hand covered hers, its warmth calming and exciting at the same time. Her heart rate sped up, but it wasn't from fear or anxiety. No, this was even more frightening. This was a spine-tingling sexual attraction in its purest form. She wanted to pull her hand away. She wanted to stand there with him touching her forever.

"I'm sorry. I'm just starting to get worried about Alex. He's never been gone this long without checking in," he said, and then his eyes met hers and locked. "That's all it is."

Without waiting for her to say anything, he lifted his hand and walked past her, leaving her to wonder what exactly had just happened. Had he not felt that? Did she just imagine a spark between the two of them? Was it just her own mixed-up emotions that had tricked her into thinking something had passed between them when he'd touched her? It had to be.

Dylan shut the door of the office before running his hands through his hair. Why had he touched her? He'd decided he wouldn't let himself get caught up in his desire to protect Katie, but she brought out all of the old instincts he felt when someone he cared for needed to be comforted. Only, it wasn't just his protectiveness causing him problems. Ever since the other night, when she'd shown up on his doorstep with her eyes sparkling with excitement over a simple white bird, he could think of nothing but her.

He'd hoped it was merely one of those small attractions that would pass. He'd get to know her, spend some more time with her, and all the excitement he felt when she was around would fade. But after touching her hand, feeling her soft skin against his rough calluses, he was afraid that it could be more than the usual male and female sexual attraction.

And he didn't need more. He had all the stress he could handle with Violet and his job. He didn't need to get involved with any woman, especially not one that was only passing through. One like Lilly, who would only complicate his life with feelings and desires that he knew had no future.

Not that he'd known that about Lilly until the day she had explained to him what they had was just a passing fling and that it was time for her to move on to her next great adventure.

Pulling out his phone, he tried to get Alex, but the phone went to voice mail again. Whatever was going on with his friend, it was keeping him busy.

Which reminded Dylan of all the things he needed to get done himself before he left to pick up Violet from her after-school care.

Turning on his computer, he started work on the monthly reports that needed to be filed with the corporate office. But no matter how he tried to focus on the screen in front of him, his mind kept wandering back to Katie.

He picked up his phone.

Are you sleeping?

He only had to wait a few seconds for her response.

No, why?

He tried to think of an excuse for disturbing her, then remembered his conversation with his daughter than morning.

Violet asked this morning if she could come over tomorrow after school.

Sure.

Okay, I'll let her know.

He forced himself to set the phone down on the desk then grabbed it up as soon as it dinged with a new message.

I'm sorry I gave you a hard time. It's just hard feeling as if there is someone hovering over you all the time.

What do you mean?

You can't deny that if it wasn't for me having been shot that you wouldn't be checking up on me. Everyone acts like I'm a different person after the shooting. My home crew, my family, everyone acts like I could have a breakdown at any point. I'm not made of glass. I worked hard to get back up in the air. I'm a good flight nurse.

He stared at the screen while he tried to figure out the best way to respond to her text. He could take her side. Agree that she should be treated as she had been before. Or he could play the devil's advocate and give her the opportunity to open up more.

But doesn't everything that happens to us change us in some way? Having Violet come into my life has changed me in ways I never imagined.

But that was a good change. You didn't mind changing because you love your daughter. It's not the same. No one acts like you can't handle yourself because you're a single father now? Not that it isn't hard. It has to be.

So you're saying you haven't changed at all? Or are you saying you don't like the changes?

When she didn't respond, he put his phone down. He hadn't meant to take their conversation into such murky waters. Hopefully he hadn't scared her away with his questions, because his instincts were telling him that she needed to talk to someone. And as a paramedic, he'd bet money on his instincts every time.

CHAPTER FIVE

THE ONLY REASON Katie had agreed to come to the party was because she knew if she didn't show up, Dylan would want to know why, which would just lead to more questions she didn't want to deal with. Now looking at the crowd of people that were there, she considered disappearing back over to her own cottage and locking the doors.

Almost the whole Key West flight crew, along with other local emergency responders, had turned out. Dylan's deck, much bigger than the one at her cottage, was overflowing with men and women, some still dressed in uniforms from jobs they'd just left.

In the middle of the deck two large pots were being heated on top of open flames where she had just been told several pounds of shrimp and crabs would soon be boiling.

She'd managed to keep to the edge of the crowd so far, not daring to chance any reaction she might have if she suddenly felt penned by the large and rowdy group.

"It can be a bit much, can't it?" said Jo, a flight nurse from the Key West crew, who had joined Katie the moment she'd walked through the back gate. "I mean, the amount of testosterone at these cookouts can be over-the-top. Take that clown over there."

Jo pointed to a man who had rolled up his shirtsleeves to show all the other men his "guns."

"He's one of the flight crew I met at shift change last week. Casey, right? Boyfriend?" Katie asked.

"Casey, also known as 'Casanova' Johnson. He's my best friend, not my boyfriend," Jo said.

But Katie noticed that the young woman's eyes lingered on her handsome friend a little more than she would have considered just friendly.

"I grew up with four brothers. That," Katie said, as they both looked on where a bunch of grown men were arguing over a game of cornhole, "was my life when I was growing up."

"You poor thing. And still you made it out alive." Jo shook her head at the scene where the men were now making wagers on what had been a friendly game.

"It wasn't so bad. I learned a lot from them. And I never had to worry about the bully at school." Katie counted herself lucky to have such supportive brothers, even though she hadn't leveled with them on how messed up her mind was before she'd left town.

"Hey, Katie. Hey, Jo," Violet greeted them.

It surprised Katie to see how Dylan's daughter seemed to gravitate to the adults at the party, though there were some other children playing in a side yard away from the hot boiling pots. She'd spent a lot of time with the little girl after school in the last week and Violet acted a bit more mature than what Katie would have expected from a child her age. And questions. The child was so full of them.

"What's new, Miss Violet?" Jo said.

"Not much. I checked out another book on birds from the library yesterday, but you weren't home, Katie. Want to come inside and see it?"

"Sure," Katie said. She gladly excused herself from the noisy crowd. Violet led her into a house whose layout was very much like her own rental. The rooms had been enlarged and the colors were much brighter, something she was sure could be attributed to Violet's influence, but it was basically the same layout.

"My room is this way," Violet said, leading her down the hallway and into a room of rose pink where the little girl climbed up on the bed and opened a large book. "See, there's more pictures in this book than the other one."

Sitting down beside the little girl, Katie studied the picture of a majestic white bird with long black legs and a bright yellow beak then read the name listed at the bottom of the page. "It's a lovely painting. I'm hoping to finish some of my own paintings before I go home."

Katie had shared some of her sketches and paintings with the little girl on her almost daily visits after school.

"Daddy says that there are a lot of birds

here because they like the sun and the sand, just like him. He knows a lot of things about the islands. He says it's because he's lived here all his life," Violet said as she turned the pages of the book to another bird. "Have you lived in New York all your life?"

"All of my life. I even lived in the same house until I got out of college and started working in my first hospital," Katie told the little girl. "How about you?"

"We lived in all kinds of places before my momma brought me here to meet my daddy. Once we even lived in this school bus that a friend of hers had fixed up." The little girl jumped down off her bed and went into her closet, coming out seconds later with a large shoebox. "Momma left these with me so that I could remember all the places we went together."

As the little girl pulled out maps and brochures, postcards and pictures, it became obvious to Katie that during Violet's short life she had traveled all across the country. From the number of locations Violet said she had lived she couldn't have been in any one place for more than a few months. What had that been like for the little girl? Always moving.

Never settling down long enough to make friends.

And now she was here in a different world without her mother.

Yet somehow, the little girl seemed to be taking all the changes in her life well. Wouldn't it be nice to be as adaptable as a child?

"I wondered where you two were. The food's ready." Dylan's voice came from the doorway.

Looking up from a picture Violet was showing her of a beach in California where the little girl spent her sixth birthday, Katie was struck once again by the fact that Dylan Maddox was the most striking man she had ever seen. Dressed in casual shorts and a button-up shirt, she couldn't look away if she wanted to.

How was it that some woman hadn't grabbed this man up by now? Or maybe they had. She didn't really know much about his past or what part Violet's mother had played in it.

"Violet has been showing me some memorabilia of her adventures," Katie said, sitting up on the bed where she and Violet had been lounging. "She's very well-traveled. I think she's been in more states than I have."

"I know. Everyone says that," Violet said, as she jumped off her bed and headed out the door.

Katie followed her and paused in the hall, where Dylan was waiting. "Nice party."

"Thanks. It's good to get the group together. We all work so closely and a lot of us grew up together," Dylan said as he followed her down the hallway.

"Violet says you've lived in the Keys all your life. Do your parents live close by?" she asked, then realized she sounded like his daughter. The little girl's inquisitiveness was rubbing off on her. Or was it just that she was curious about Dylan?

"I grew up in Islamorada on a houseboat in a marina my parents owned," Dylan said.

"A houseboat? You lived in the water?" She couldn't imagine it.

"It was a perfectly fine boat. I had a loft bedroom until I was in middle school when my mother insisted that my father build a house beside the marina. They still live there, though if my dad had his way they'd be back on the houseboat."

"You and Violet have lived such adventurous lives," she said as he started to open one of the French doors leading out onto the balcony.

"Violet had more than enough adventure by the time I found out about her," Dylan muttered as he stopped in front of the door.

"What do you mean, when you found out about her? You didn't know you had a daughter?"

"Not until her mother showed up with her. She never told me she was pregnant. I think she panicked when she found out she was having Violet. I think she thought I would hold her here if I knew about the baby. One night I came home and she was packed up and on her way out the door. I don't know if I would have ever heard from her again if it hadn't been for Violet."

She could see the pain in his eyes as he spoke about his past, but she didn't know if it was because of the time he'd lost with his daughter or the way he'd been treated by Violet's mother.

"Violet was getting too old to be dragged from school to school. She's a smart child and even at eight she knew that she needed to attend a school on a regular basis. That's hard to do when your mother can't seem to stay in the same place more than four months at a time."

She didn't hear the bitterness she would have expected toward his ex. Could it be that he still had feelings for Violet's mother? Or maybe he'd just accepted the past and moved on?

She found herself wanting to know the answer to those questions.

"Violet's very lucky that she made it back to you. You're doing a great job with her. I would never have known she'd been in and out of different schools from the way she was reading that book on birds to me."

"She's been the center of my world since she moved here. I wish I could have been there when she was born, but… I can't undo that," Dylan said as he went back to opening the door then stopped again. "What I've never understood is why Lilly thought that I would make her stay somewhere she didn't want to be. I'd never do that to a woman."

"Of course you wouldn't," Katie said as they stepped out into the crowd, though it was the last thing she wanted to do. She had forgotten about all the other people being here while she'd been talking to Violet and then Dylan.

For the rest of the evening, she made excuses for going in and out of the house as she carried out drinks and gathered up trash. At other times, she'd wander off into the garden and pretend to be studying the bright blooms if someone came too close.

Since she didn't have the drive home that the other guests did, she offered to stay and help clean up. She'd learned several things as the night continued, besides all the ways to avoid a crowd of people. One, crab boils were messy and delicious, and two, the group of hardworking emergency responders were all loud and competitive, much like the men and women she was used to working with in NYC.

The quiet that descended after the last guest left was very welcomed. Violet had been put to bed earlier in the night, leaving Katie alone with Dylan.

"This is the last of it," she said as she walked into the house where they had been loading the dishwasher with utensils and serving plates.

"Thanks for staying to help," Dylan said.

"Just trying to make points with my boss," Katie teased, knowing that the man hated to be referred to as anyone's boss.

"I'm not your boss, I'm a fill-in. I think of myself more as your preceptor," Dylan said as he took the last dish from her.

"I don't need a preceptor. I've been the preceptor for more crew members than you have staff here." She tried to keep the bite out of her voice, but she was getting tired of being treated like a newbie. Her pride had taken enough of a hit after she'd been injured on the job. She didn't need someone making her feel even more of a failure. She thought he understood that.

"Okay, let's say I'm more of your mentor. Everyone needs a mentor at some point, right?" he said.

He turned around and was leaning against the black granite countertops. Why was he so determined to help her? And why did it infuriate her so?

But when she didn't say anything, he moved closer. His hand came up and pushed a lock of hair that had come loose from her ponytail behind her ear.

The room was quiet except for the hum of the air-conditioning unit. Her heart began to race and her breaths came more quickly. Her thoughts turned back to the first time they had met in the flight quarter's kitchen when his arms had come around her and her body had immediately reacted. They'd both been strangers then. In some ways, they still were.

"I didn't mean to make you feel inept. Your record shows that you're a good flight nurse."

She tried to concentrate on his words, on the anger she had felt earlier. But it was gone. All she could think about was his touch, his body so close to hers. What would he do if she moved closer? If she reached up with her lips and touched his?

Her hand went up and pressed against his chest before she could stop it. His heart beat a fast rhythm against her palm as hers did when he covered her hand with his own.

"Do you feel it?" she asked him.

What was she doing? This wasn't her. She didn't approach men. Not like this. Instead, she waited until they showed an interest in her before expressing her own.

"Katie, I…yes, if you mean do I want

to take you in my arms and kiss you, and more, right now. Yes. There's an attraction between the two of us, but..." Dylan took a deep breath then stepped back from her, leaving her feeling empty and alone. "You're only here for a few weeks. I make it a rule not to get involved with anyone that's only here temporarily."

At first his words didn't make sense to her and then she thought of his daughter. "Because of Violet? Or because of Lilly?"

"I'm still trying to get this whole father thing down. But yes, it's best if we don't confuse Violet." Dylan took another step away from her.

Was that disappointment she saw? Or was that just her wounded pride being wishful? It didn't really matter, did it? She'd just come on to a man for the first time, only to be shot down. And he'd been her, sort of, boss. There wasn't anything that was going to make this any less awkward.

"If you think you can handle the rest of this, I'm going to head home." As she turned toward the entrance, she tried to leave with her chin up. How was she going to face this man the next day? Or the next? She'd made a really bad misstep here and she didn't know how to recover. She didn't want Dylan's pity. She'd had enough of that after being shot. It had made her feel weak and helpless, two things McGees never accepted.

"Katie—" Dylan caught her hand as she started to open the door "—don't leave. Not like this."

She made herself turn around. She made her lips curve in a smile, made her eyes hold back the embarrassing tears that she felt forming. She wouldn't let him know he had hurt her. Besides, it wasn't his fault that he didn't have the same feelings that she did.

"My daughter gets attached to people very easily and she's spent most of her life having to leave the people in her life behind as her mother dragged her from one city to the next. And then her own mother left her. I'm not likely to bring a woman into our home for a long while."

"I understand. It's not a big deal. I just..." What could she use as an excuse for that stupid confession of her attraction to him? "I'm sorry. I was out of line. I understand that things are more complicated for you now."

And with that admission she was out the

door and halfway back to her rental before she could say anything else that would embarrass the two of them and make things even worse. Not that she thought they could. Not when she had to get up in the morning and face Dylan again with the both of them knowing that there was an attraction between them even though he couldn't act on it.

Dylan had finished cleaning up and was headed to bed when he glanced out his window and saw that Katie's light was still on.

He had so many mixed feelings where she was concerned. He was almost glad that she had forced him to admit his attraction to her, though he didn't know why. It certainly hadn't made it easier to let her walk away when all he'd wanted to do was take her into his arms and kiss her the way he had dreamed of since the night she'd shown up on his front porch with that smile that had awakened something inside him.

And now he'd hurt her, even though that had been the last of his intentions. And he'd ignored her suggestion that it was his feelings for Lilly that kept him from becoming involved with her.

He pulled his phone out of his pocket. At least that was something he could set straight.

It's not Lilly. At least not any feelings I have left for her.

It only took a second for her to respond.

Are you sure?

Yes. After she left I was pretty messed up. I didn't understand how she could just walk away like that. It was hard on my ego to accept that I had only been someone to pass the time with while Lilly planned her next big adventure. While I'd been making plans for the future, she'd been on her way out the door.

You were hurt. It's understandable.

I was young and innocent then.

You make yourself sound like an old man.

I feel old sometimes.

When she didn't text back, he went to bed. He was just turning off the lights when his phone dinged.

Thank you for telling me. I'm not like Lilly, but I do understand you wanting to protect your daughter. You're right. Things would never work between the two of us. I've only got six more weeks before I return to New York. I wouldn't want to hurt Violet when I left.

She didn't have to say that she wouldn't want to hurt him either. It was understood.

Good night, Katie.

Good night, Dylan.

The radio went off waking Katie up with a start from her nap in her quarters. She had her flight suit and shoes on and was rushing out the door before she could open her eyes enough to check the time, and she was surprised to see the sun coming up when she climbed into the helicopter. She was even more surprised to find Dylan occupying the seat beside her.

"Where's Max?" she asked as she buckled herself into her seat. There wasn't really time for idle conversation, but she couldn't help but be confused. When she'd gone to bed at 2 a.m. after a call for a scooter accident victim who needed to be flown to a Miami hospital where a plastic surgeon would try to fix the patient's many facial fractures, Max had been there.

"I came in early and found him in the lounge nursing a headache and upset stomach. I told him I'd cover till the next shift came on." As Dylan was going through their scene bag, she noticed that he was adding more bandages.

"I missed hearing the dispatch. What's the call?" she asked.

"Self-inflicted gunshot wound to the head. Fire and rescue on scene clearing a space in the parking lot of Zachary Taylor fort. EMS is on the scene with the patient," Roy said over the headset. "ETA eight minutes."

Her stomach clenched at the word *gunshot* and refused to relax. "Are we sure it was self-inflicted?"

"We'll let the police make that judgment,"

Dylan said. "Are you okay? You aren't coming down with what Max has, are you?"

"I'm fine," she said, determined not to let her mind get ahead of her. This would be fine. She just needed to keep her mind off the fact that someone had been shot. Instead, she would concentrate on their patient, who would need all of their attention if they were going to keep them alive long enough to get to a neurosurgeon, which was about all they could do for this type of head injury.

She spiked a bag of Lactated Ringer's. She considered also preparing a bag of the O negative blood that they had recently begun stocking for traumas such as this one, but she decided this would be a fast "drop, package and load" job so it would be best to wait until the patient was strapped in and headed to the hospital before starting a transfusion.

In what seemed like seconds, they were landing in a parking lot that had been blocked off by the other emergency responders. The second the skids touched down they were out and moving toward a firefighter who she recognized from the earlier scene that morning.

"He's this way," the man said as they followed him down a sandy path that led them out to a beach where she could see EMS working on their patient. Katie looked around the scene, anxiety sending a boost of adrenaline through her.

They were in the open, with only a small group of early-morning runners gathered around a young woman dressed in a tank top and runner shorts who was visibly upset. Was this the person who had found him? Or had she seen the man pull the trigger?

Or was this really a suicide? Could there be a shooter in the crowd? Her stomach churned at the thought.

She was being paranoid. There was no risk here. *I'm safe*, Katie told herself. *This is not New York. There is no place for a shooter to hide here.*

A police officer stood close to the EMS, snapping pictures of the crime scene. It only took one look at the sand beside the patient to notice a small revolver.

The sight of the gun and the smell of gunpowder set her stomach churning again. She could see the pool of blood under the man's head as it soaked into the wet sand.

For a moment she was back in New York

as she watched her own blood as it flowed onto the asphalt, mixing with the rainwater that streamed across the parking lot. It was the sight of her own blood that she remembered the most about that night.

"We need to get an airway before he goes into respiratory arrest. Katie, you help them with that bandage and keep his head supported while I get this guy intubated," Dylan told her, breaking the hold of fear that had gripped her.

"Sure, okay," she said and moved to help support the man's injured head as a collar was secured around his neck. They were unable to see an exit wound, so it was possible the bullet had traveled into his cervical spine.

In the next few minutes it took to get the man packaged and loaded in the helicopter, Katie ignored everything that was going on around her except for what was happening with her patient.

Once they were back in the air and headed toward Miami, she quickly got a second IV line started as Dylan started the neurological assessment. The cabin was quiet while they worked together to stabilize their patient.

"He's going into shock. I'm going to increase the fluids and start some blood," she told Dylan as she took the first unit of O negative blood out of the cooler and began the task of prepping it. Once she had the tubing attached and primed, she hooked it into the second line she'd started and opened it up. After seeing the amount of blood at the scene, there'd been no doubt that this man had lain there and bled for a while before someone had come along and found him. If it had been another thirty minutes their services wouldn't have been needed. Even with their help in getting him to a trauma unit that could provide neurosurgery, his chances weren't very good.

"Pupils are fixed and dilated. Glasgow Coma Scale of five," Dylan said as he started his report to the Miami trauma unit.

In minutes they were landing and unloading their patient. As they entered the overcrowded emergency room, she took over manually ventilating the patient so that Dylan could give report to the trauma doc that had been waiting for them.

They both made quick work of transferring their patient onto the trauma stretcher where he was immediately surrounded by qualified staff that would try to keep the man alive. After washing down the stretcher, they stopped in the lounge set up for the emergency responders and they each fueled up with a cup of coffee before heading back to the helipad with a cup of the thick, black liquid for Roy.

The flight back to base was quiet. Dylan didn't comment on her loss of concentration at the scene earlier and she was not going to be the one to bring it up. She'd made it through the flight and he couldn't find any fault with her patient care.

"What's the chance of that guy making it?" Roy asked them once they had landed.

"Better than the chances he had if we hadn't been there to transfer him," Dylan said.

"That's what you always say," Roy said.

"Because it's always true, though for this guy I don't know that there's much they're going to be able to do for him," Dylan said.

"It's a shame, isn't it?" Roy said. "That guy was so young."

"No one knows what demons drive someone to do the things they do. If he's lucky and survives this, the hospital will make sure he gets some help," Dylan said as he opened the door and they all walked in to find their relief enjoying a breakfast of eggs and bacon. "I hope you cooked enough for all of us."

"I'm not hungry. I think I'll just head home." Katie hurried toward her room to get her backpack. It had been a long twenty-four-hour shift and she wanted to get out of there before Dylan had a chance to corner her. She was sure they'd eventually talk about what had happened at the scene that morning, but she wasn't up to dealing with it now.

"Katie," she heard his voice call from behind her. They'd avoided each other the past week while at home. It seemed best after the awkward incident the night of the party. Unfortunately, avoiding him wasn't really an option here at work.

"Hey," Dylan said, catching up with her, "are you okay?"

"I'm fine. Just tired." She wasn't about to admit to him how much seeing that gunshot victim had triggered something inside her. She'd held it together. Maybe he hadn't noticed how she had become too absorbed in her own reactions to the scene this morning.

"Good, I won't hold you up, then. I hate to ask you this, but I was wondering if you could do me a favor."

Katie stopped where she stood, the doorknob of her assigned room in her hand, unable to imagine what Dylan could want from her. Was he going to ask her to keep away from him and Violet when she was home so he didn't have to worry about her attraction to him? It hadn't just been her avoiding him. She'd noticed there hadn't been any trips by Violet over to her house.

"Okay," she said as she prepared herself. No matter what it was, she would be professional. She had a room full of coworkers just outside that hallway. She still had some pride left.

"I just got a call from my babysitter who's been keeping Violet for me this week so I can work later and she can't make it today. Would it be okay if Violet came over this afternoon when she gets off the bus? It will only be for an hour. I've got a late online meeting that I don't want to miss."

Katie let go of the breath she was holding and for the first time that day she felt a smile tug at her lips. "Of course I can watch Violet.

I'm going home to take a nap this morning, but I'll be up by the time she gets home. I've seen the bus out there so I know the time, though you might want to send a note to the school just so there's not a problem with me getting her."

"Thanks, Katie. I appreciate it. And Violet has been giving me fits about wanting to come visit you."

After assuring Dylan that she would enjoy her visit with Violet, she grabbed her things and quickly left the building.

But it was impossible for her to sleep. She worried about how the scene that morning had not only affected her but kept winding its way through her mind. She'd fought her way back to being physically capable of doing her job, and while she knew that the patient's care had not been compromised by her reaction, she had to admit that it had left her shaken.

Getting out of bed, she sent an email to the counselor she'd been avoiding. It was time she faced her own demons. As much as she tried, she had to accept that she couldn't just pretend everything was okay. She had tried to ignore all the signs, but the flight this morning had scared her. It had been a wake-up call.

CHAPTER SIX

DYLAN HEARD THE laughter coming from Katie's back porch. He would recognize the giggles of his little girl anywhere. But there was another sound, one that he wasn't sure he'd ever heard before. The sound of Katie's laughter was as pleasant as Violet's and it warmed something inside of him.

Ever since the night he had admitted his attraction to Katie, he'd felt as if a part of himself had turned cold and distant. As if inside him was another man, one who wasn't happy with his decision to turn Katie away.

Which made absolutely no sense. It hadn't been the first time he'd explained his solid rule on not dating someone who was just passing through his life. It had never bothered him before. And now, with Violet, he had even more reasons uphold this rule. Unlike her mother, he knew that Violet needed a stable home, which didn't include people rotating in and out of her life.

Still, he knew something about the way he reacted to Katie was different or could be different if he let them have a chance.

A crash came from the deck and he picked up speed. What were the two of them doing that would have furniture crashing to the floor?

The sight of Violet and Katie collapsed on the ground did nothing to ease his fears until he realized they were both rolling around in a fit of giggles instead of pain.

"What exactly are the two of you up to?" he asked. Standing over them, he couldn't help but join in the laughter.

"Katie is teaching me yoga. It's supposed to lighten us," his little girl said.

"Enlighten us," Katie corrected. "So far all it's gotten us is a couple of bruises. Violet is having some difficulty with the meditation part of the process."

"Katie says you can't talk during the meditation. It's supposed to help you relax. But how can you relax if you can't talk?" his daughter asked, genuine confusion reflected on her little pixie face.

"I can understand where that would be very stressful," he agreed with his daughter before looking over at Katie and giving her a wink.

"We decided it was best to move on to learning the yoga positions. Violet is a lot better at those." Katie gave his daughter a look of affection that completely warmed his heart. Could Katie see what a special little girl his daughter was? Violet was a beautiful and loving child, but sometimes she could be a bit much, at least for some adults.

"We've done the downward dog and now we're learning the cow pose. Only I told Katie that it looked more like a dog than the other one. And then—" Violet had to stop to giggle before she could talk again "—Katie started mooing like a cow and it made me laugh so I fell over."

"I was not mooing. I was moaning from all the stretching my muscles were doing. They're not used to being mistreated," Katie said.

She was sitting with her back to the overturned chair, her hair plastered with sweat against her flushed face. He picked up two bottles of water sitting on the table and handed one to each of them. “It’s a bit hot out here. Couldn’t you do this in the house?”

“It said on the website that being outside was good for meditating.” Katie took a gulp of water. “I should have waited till the sun went down. But we did have fun, didn’t we, Violet?”

Violet agreed with a nod as she drank her water.

“So, you’ve never done yoga?” he asked. Looking down at the khaki dress pants he’d had to put on for the county commissioners meeting he had been required to attend on Alex’s absence then looked at the deck. Deciding to take the chance of ruining his pants, he sat down on the floor between the two.

“No. My counselor recommended it, so I thought I would give it a try. If nothing else, I’ve learned that I need to get into better shape. And Violet definitely made it more fun than it could have been.”

Her admission that she’d been in contact with her counselor surprised him. She’d seemed so set against getting counseling before. What had changed?

Was it her reaction to the gunshot scene this morning? He had intended to discuss it with her the next day when she reported to work. He'd seen her go pale when she saw the gun and blood. It made sense that something like that could trigger bad memories. It had troubled him all day, but he wanted her to have some time to recover before he brought it up.

"I had fun, too, Katie. Can I come practice with you another day?" his daughter asked. "I'll find a book in the library about doing yoga for us to study."

"Of course. How about I order us a CD to use?" Katie said.

As she moved to get up, he stood and offered her his hand. He couldn't help but notice the hesitation before she took it. Was he making things between them even more awkward with his presence?

"Is it okay if I go home and finish my homework? I forgot to bring my library book to school and I need to finish my report," Violet said.

"Actually, your nana is on her way to pick you up so you can spend the night with her."

"Really?" his daughter asked.

"She'll be here in just a few minutes so you better go get your clothes and books together. I've already opened the door. I'll be there to help in a minute."

"It's okay. I can get my stuff. Thanks, Katie," Violet called back as she dashed off.

"I'll have to go check her bag. She'll remember her favorite books, but she'll forget to pack her pajamas." He watched his daughter until she disappeared into the house. "I really appreciate you keeping her for me."

"Actually, it helped me a lot. After this morning, it was nice to have a distraction. You're very lucky. Violet's a special little girl. She has an abundance of spirit and energy," Katie said, though he noticed she was looking down at her shoes instead of looking him in the eyes. "About this morning,"

"We can talk about this morning tomorrow." The last thing he wanted was to create any more conflict between the two of them. He'd rather leave what happened at work, at work.

And why was that when he'd been the one

to tell her that the two of them couldn't get any closer?

"No. I want to discuss it. Whilst the patient's care was not compromised, I need to talk about how the accident in New York affected me"

"Katie, you got caught up in your surroundings. Our patient wasn't affected. You need to realize that you're human like the rest of us. You should have seen me when Lilly showed up with Violet. I was a mess. Trying to figure out how I was going to take care of a seven-year-old daughter while keeping up with my job was too much some days."

"Really?" she asked, her eyes meeting his for the first time. "But you look so comfortable with her."

"Now? Yes, I've got a handle on things, though I know that could change at any time. I live in fear that Lilly will show up and want her back. And she's growing up so fast. In a few years I'll have a teenager to deal with." The thought of his little girl turning into a young woman was enough to send a shudder down his spine.

"You'll do fine. Violet has a good head on her shoulders," Katie said. She bit down on her bottom lip, drawing his eyes down to plump red lips that he had imagined kissing. He wanted to touch them, brush his fingers across their softness before he lost himself in a kiss he knew would shake the foundations of his closely held beliefs that getting involved with her would only be asking for heartache later for both him and his daughter when she returned to New York.

"Besides, if you have full custody the courts won't let her take Violet," Katie said. "You do have custody, right?"

His stomach clenched into a tight ball as it always did when the question of Violet's custody came up. "That's the problem. Lilly was only here for a day before she was gone. There wasn't time for me to get anything but emergency temporary custody. If she came back and wanted to contest, I'm not sure what would happen."

"That doesn't make sense. Her mother left her. She apparently doesn't want to be responsible for Violet. Can't your lawyer just send the paperwork for her to sign?"

"Sounds simple, right? The only problem is that by the time we find out where Lilly is living, she moves again. We've even used private detectives, but she's always one step in front of us. If I didn't know better I'd think that she was trying to avoid us." And he was beginning to think that he was right which only made him more paranoid concerning his daughter's safety.

"I'm sorry. I didn't know. I'm sure that it will work out. You're doing such a good job with her I'm sure that the court would never think of taking custody away from you."

Katie's hand reached for his in what he knew was intended as a comforting gesture that shouldn't make his heart jump, but it did. And it wasn't only his heart that was reacting. His whole body seemed to buzz with excitement.

"I hope so. I'm lucky that I have a lot of support from our team and my family." He needed to leave. He needed to get away from those lips and her touch before the temptation had him throwing out all his remaining caution and taking a chance on what could be between the two of them—even if only for a few weeks.

"Daddy, Nana just drove up," Violet shouted from somewhere behind him, breaking him from the spell that Katie's tempting lips had cast over him.

"I'll be right there," he called back to her. "We'll talk tomorrow," he said, eager to make his escape. He'd almost forgotten what she wanted to talk to him about.

"Sure," Katie said, stepping back.

It wasn't until she backed away from him that he realized he had taken a step toward her. As he made his way across the yard to his home, he couldn't help but wonder what would have happened if Violet hadn't interrupted him? Would he have touched her? Kissed her? Or would he have stepped away as he knew he should?

Something told him there would come a time again when he would have to make that decision, when his daughter wouldn't be there to rescue him, and he had no idea how he would hand it. It seemed all his rules, no matter how important they had seemed to him just weeks ago, were crumbling around him.

After a long shower, Katie pulled on a pair of pajama shorts and a tank top before taking a glass of her favorite Moscato wine out to the deck. After sitting up the chair she and Violet had knocked over earlier in the afternoon, she took a seat and closed her eyes. A soft breeze from the beach ruffled her hair that she had left down to dry and the sweet scent of the hibiscus plants that edged the deck on both sides filled the air, relaxing her even more.

She'd been forced to accept some hard truths today, but she felt better for it. Like her father had always told her, it was better to face a problem head-on than to sweep it under the table and ignore it. She'd done a lot of sweeping over the last few months. She'd been willing to do whatever physical work was required to get back to work as a flight nurse, but she'd ignored all the physiological signs her body had been giving her each time she found herself in a situation that reminded her of her own traumatic injury. She'd made excuses and pretended that all she needed was to run away to Florida and she would leave all her problems behind. If only it was that easy.

But it wasn't. There was nothing easy about her life right now. Her counselor said she had to accept what happened to her and voice it out loud, and Katie finally thought she understood the reason she'd hid it all behind her. Because it hadn't been just an injury as she had tried to pretend, it had been a violent attack with a gun. She'd been shot by an unknown assailant while trying to do her job and save the life of a young patient. And after living a life where she'd always felt safe, the admission of being vulnerable was hard to accept. It was time for her stop ignoring the pain and fear that she experienced that night. And it was time to stop pretending she was okay. She had to acknowledge that she was no superhero, she was simply one of many people who had gone through a trauma that would probably affect them the rest of their lives.

If she wanted to return to New York in better condition than when she'd left, she had to make a conscious effort to accept what she was going through and find a way to overcome the fear and anxiety that were controlling her. Before the shooting, she'd attended some of the most violent scenes imaginable as she tried to save patients who had been beaten, shot, stabbed and worse. Even when her heart was torn apart by the suffering of her patients, she was able to separate her feelings from her job to provide the best care. Now she had to find in herself the strength to separate from her own trauma, so she could go on with her life while still accepting that her life had changed forever. No, she wouldn't forget it, she'd come to realize that wasn't possible, but she could learn to live with it.

And she had to figure out what she wanted out of her life. She'd always put her job first, which was why instead of caring about her mental health she had concentrated more on her physical rehab after the shooting. Coming from a family committed to helping others, she'd lost sight of the fact that there could be more to her life. That was going to change too.

Watching Dylan and Violet and their relationship had affirmed for her the possibility of enjoying a life beyond work.

She opened her eyes and reached for the glass of wine on the side table and froze. A large green dragon looked up at her from the floor of the deck, its long, forked tongue shooting out toward her. She screamed.

* * *

Dylan just finished cleaning up the kitchen when a bloodcurdling scream tore through the silence of his home. Grabbing his keys and phone, he power-locked his front door before shooting across the yard to Katie.

Her cottage was quiet when he let himself in. Too quiet. He cleared each room before he got to the doors leading out to the deck. He could see by the outside string of lights that she sat straight up in the chair, her eyes fixed on something that was at her feet. Easing the door open, he made sure there was no one out of his field of sight before he took a step outside, only realizing then that he didn't have a weapon to defend her.

"Katie, what happened?" he asked calmly. Had she had a flashback? Fallen asleep and dreamed of the night she'd been shot?

"It's a dragon," Katie whispered, her voice quivering. "It's between my feet."

Her words confused him. A dragon? And then it hit him. New York City girls wouldn't have a lot of experience interacting with the kind of local wildlife they had here on the islands.

"Is this dragon green or brown?" He tried to keep the laughter out of his words.

"It's green and it's big. It's evil too. I can see it in its little beady black eyes. It tried to strike me with its tongue," Katie said, never moving her eyes off the creature that he could now see on the deck beside her feet.

"It's okay. It's just an iguana. They don't bite." He started toward her when what he saw stopped him.

"I've seen iguanas. This thing is too big to be an iguana. It's a monster. It looks like something that would fight Godzilla."

While he heard her words, he couldn't seem to find his voice to respond. He'd been prepared to see a three-foot iguana with a spikey row of spines on its back and its long thick tail. What he hadn't been prepared for was the sight of Katie in a pair of short shorts and a tank top that revealed everything it was supposed to be covering. He struggled to regain his voice. "Don't move. I'm going to get some oven mitts from the kitchen to pick it up."

"No, Dylan, wait. Don't leave me alone with this thing." Katie's voice was louder now. "Do something before it moves. What if it jumps on me? It's got claws."

Dylan headed back into the kitchen. "It's an herbivore. It won't bite you unless you make it mad, so don't make it mad."

"And how do I keep it from getting mad?" Katie asked, her voice getting higher and louder now.

"I don't know. Maybe you should talk to it?" Unable to find a pair of oven mitts he settled on a couple of pot holders and rushed back outside.

"And if you bite me I'll sic my brother John Jr. on you. He's one of NYPD's finest. He'll not only shoot you, he'll have you made into a belt to show all his friends. And if John is busy, my older brother Jacob will put a bullet between those evil eyes of yours and then..." Katie stopped her conversation with the iguana as soon as he stepped close to them.

"Sorry, I didn't mean to interrupt. I'm surprised the little fellow hasn't run off into the bushes shaking in fear from all those threats of violence." He stepped behind the iguana and with one quick movement had the three-foot-long creature caught between his hands.

The green scaly creature gave him a disgruntled look, but made no move to attack.

Katie sank back into her chair. "What in the world was that thing doing out here? Where's its owner?"

"It doesn't have an owner. Haven't you seen them around the island? They're everywhere. If I'm not mistaken, this one here is named Pascal."

"Who…wait—" she held her hands up in surrender "—I know the answer to that one already. Violet named him, didn't she?"

"She did. Hold on a moment. I'm going to take him over to our back garden. He usually doesn't stray too far from there."

When he got back to the deck he found Katie hadn't moved, but her glass of wine was now empty and she held her phone in her hand. "Are you all right? I know iguanas look scary, but as long as you leave them alone they won't bite you."

"Oh, you don't have to worry. I will definitely leave them alone. Unfortunately, they're not the problem right now. It's the text I just got from my brother. It seems my father wants to hear from me." Katie started to take a drink from the glass before realizing it was empty and setting it down on the table.

"And that's a problem?" he asked. Wasn't it natural for a father to want to check in on his daughter?

But what did he really know about Katie's family life? Katie hadn't talk a lot about her life in New York. Had she been married before? Did she have someone waiting there for her? No, she wouldn't have responded to him the way she had if there was someone else. But why had it never occurred to him to ask?

Because you told her there couldn't be anything between the two of you.

"Let's just say that Captain John McGee Sr. of the NYPD is the man in charge of the McGee clan. If he wants to talk to me, there's something on his mind. He's probably checking up on me, making sure I'm doing a good job while I'm here."

"You haven't called him since you've been here?" he asked. Was this what he had to look forward to when Violet grew up?

"We've texted," Katie said.

"But you haven't called?" He could tell by the way her eyes shot down that there were some feelings of guilt there which made her admission even more surprising. “Because as a dad, I can tell you that receiving some texts would not be enough for me if Violet was away from home.”

“I know it’s hard on you. Thinking about the time Violet was out there in the world without you being there to protect her.”

“If I’d only received one phone call telling me she existed, that she was out there, I would have found some way to get to her.” Dylan’s hands ran through his hair as he was filled with the familiar frustration that he couldn’t go back and change things for Violet’s first years.

“It’s just…my father’s a big teddy bear of a man as long as everything is going his way. When it’s not, that’s when things get a little intense. He’s got a protective streak a mile long, especially for me since I’m the only girl, but he has high expectations for all his children. My brothers followed him into the NYPD. I became a flight nurse. He’s proud of all of us, but he has a tendency to worry.”

“So, call him. Put his mind to rest. Let him know you’re good. I can understand his concern.”

“But I’m not. Doing well that is. I didn’t

even tell him the truth about why I came down to Key West. He has no idea I was struggling at work after the shooting. I've never told him. I've never told anyone except for my counselor. And you."

And why was that? Maybe for the same reason that he felt so comfortable telling her about his fears for Violet's custody?

But he couldn't let himself dwell on the whys and what-ifs.

"The scene this morning was not a pleasant one. And I can see why it would have disturbed you. You're not superhuman. We all have something that digs into us on a scene. For me it's the kids. Seeing a child hurting just does something to me."

They sat in silence for a few moments. Having to treat a hurt child got to all of them.

"But let's get back to your father. What do you think your father expected after being shot? That you'd climb out of the hospital bed and head back to work. If he's been an officer long enough to be a captain, he's seen his fellow officers shot in the line of duty, which by the way is exactly what happened to you. You were on duty to take care of a patient and got shot at the scene. No one would have blamed you if you never returned to work. The fact that you fought to come back is a testament to your strength." His voice got louder as he thought about what Katie had been through, his protective nature reacting to the thought that she'd been carrying all this around alone. "I take it that's why you're not calling him. You're afraid he'll realize that there is something wrong?"

"I've never told him. About the dreams, the fear of crowds or the anxiety every time something reminds me of that night. I told him I was fine. And he told me he was proud of me. I want him to be proud of me. That's all I've ever wanted. He's been everything to me. My mom died of cancer not too long after my brother was born. I was only four. But he was a lot like you. He accepted that he was raising us alone and he made it work," Katie said as she wiped at his face. "But after this morning and after talking to my counselor, I know if I want to be the nurse that I was before the...shooting... I need to acknowledge the problem and find a way to overcome it."

"Can I ask you a question?" Dylan had pulled up on the chairs and taken a seat across from her while they'd been talking. Now he moved a little closer. "Why is it so hard to say that you were shot? I've noticed that you usually refer to it as 'the incident' or 'my injury.' Is it so hard to admit that you were shot?"

She bit down on her bottom lip and he was once more caught up in their spell. One day he would taste those lips even if he did have to break all his rules.

"I don't know. My counselor asked me the same question. She suggested it might be my way of refusing to accept that it happened. That I've been a victim of a shooting. Maybe she's right. I'm not supposed to be the victim. I'm supposed to care for the victim. I'm supposed to save the victim's life with all the special training I've received. That's my job. You know, they prepare us for the most violent scenes. The shootings and stabbings, the car accidents and the beatings, but never have I had someone explain what I'm supposed to do if *I* am the victim."

"What happened that night?" he asked. He needed to know. Not because of curiosity, but because he wanted to know what he was dealing with. He wanted to know how to help her. He ignored the warning his brain was sending him, reminding him of his vow not to get involved because that was how you ended up getting hurt. None of it mattered now. What he saw was a coworker, a friend, someone he was quickly coming to care about who needed help. He might not be a counselor, but he could be there for her when she needed someone to talk to.

"It was just a regular call. A shooting victim had been left to die in an old run-down parking lot in Jersey. EMS had responded to the call, but this kid needed to get to an operating room fast if he was going to survive. It had been raining off and on all day, so we hadn't taken any flights until we were dispatched to this one. The lights in the parking lot had been shot out or had just died. But I had on this old yellow rain jacket, so there's no way someone couldn't see me." She stood as she talked and he followed her with his eyes. She looked defenseless as she paced back and forth with her arms wrapped around her body. "I was lead so I got to the patient first. He couldn't have been over eighteen. Just a kid, you know? After that, it's all kind of confused in my mind."

"Can you try to explain it to me?" He wanted to get up and go to her. He wanted to take her into his arms and tell her that she was safe now, but that wouldn't help her deal with all the emotions she had been apparently dealing with alone. Somehow he knew she needed to voice out loud what had happened. She admitted herself that he was the only one she felt comfortable talking to.

"I don't know if I can, but I'll try. They tell me that there had been someone hiding behind the building. They, the shooter, must have come back to make sure he finished the kid off. Maybe he saw that EMS had arrived and he was afraid they were going to save the guy and then there would have been retaliation. All I really remember was bending over the kid, EMS was trying to get an IV on the guy. The lights in the parking lot were all out and none of us could see very well. Then there was a popping sound, it sounded more like fireworks then gunshots. I felt something hit me in the chest. At first I didn't feel the pain. It was just a shock. I didn't realize what was happening." She continued to pace as she talked, still holding the empty wineglass in her hand.

"They tried to make it out that I was some kind of hero, saying that I tried to protect the patient, but I don't know if I was covering the kid or if the first bullet hit me and I fell over him. There were screams, I remember hearing them, but I don't know if they were mine or if they came from someone else at the scene. Sometimes I dream that it's me screaming and sometimes I dream it's the kid screaming, though that isn't possible since he was unresponsive when we arrived."

She passed in front of him and he caught the hand that held the empty glass in his and unpeeled her fingers from the thin stem. After setting it on the table, he pulled her down into his arms until she sat in his lap.

"What are you doing?" she asked.

Her misty eyes met his and he asked himself the same question. What *was* he doing?

But his heart told him this was what he needed. He couldn't sit there and watch her go through the hell of that night again without touching her. Without reassuring himself that she was safe. She was going through something that he couldn't imagine living through. How could he help her? By being honest with her?

"Can I comfort you?" he said, then waited. He wondered if she understood just how much hearing about her pain hurt him too. How could she when it didn't even make sense to him?

Her tense body suddenly relaxed into his. Her head came down to rest on his shoulders and the helplessness he was feeling eased as he wrapped his arms around her. They sat with him just holding her there for several minutes before he felt he could speak.

"I'm so sorry you went through that. I know you think that you're not satisfied with where you are in your recovery, but the fact that you've been able to get on a helicopter not knowing what kind of scene or what danger awaits you is a sign of your resiliency." But for how long could she continue before she pushed herself too far? He couldn't, wouldn't, let her do that. The look of horror on her face when she'd seen the gunshot victim had told him that she was still struggling. He would find some way to protect her.

"But it's not enough. Nothing is enough. I want to move on. I want to forget all about that night. I want my life back," Katie said, her voice muffled against his shirt.

She wanted her life in New York back. And if he had any sense he would get up right then and walk away from this woman. But it was too late. He had no defense against the feelings she brought out of him.

"Thank you for listening. I haven't been able to talk about it. About the night I was shot," Katie said, enunciating each word as if it were a pain in itself. "I know that trying to ignore what happened that night is making it harder for me to recover, but it's not something I've felt comfortable talking about with others. My brothers…they're so angry that they haven't been able to find the person who shot me. I can't put this on them."

"I'm glad you're comfortable talking to me," he said as she raised her head from his shoulder. Her eyes had dried but they were still just as bright. Her lips, those red plump lips that had tempted him for days, were only inches from his.

When his gaze returned to hers, something passed between them. A need, a desire, like none he had ever felt before had him lowering his head as her mouth turned up toward his.

Her lips opened the second they touched

his, surprising him with her own need as their tongues tangled. Desire for more shot through him. Even though he tried to tell himself that they were moving way too fast, he had to touch her. His hands were under her tank top and the feel of her bare breasts as he cupped them sent a dangerous desire through his body. The feel of her fingers as they curled into his back of his neck, her nails sharp against his skin, was almost too much. When she wiggled her shorts-clad bottom as she readjusted herself in his lap, he groaned. If they didn't stop that moment it would be too late. Was he ready to take this step?

He was torn in half, part of him wanting more while the other was determined this couldn't go any further.

Katie had been nothing but honest with him when she'd admitted her attraction to him. And he had been honest with her about the reasons that he couldn't become involved with anyone that would be temporary in his and Violet's life. Violet had to come first. His daughter had spent too much of her life without someone looking out for her. But that was his job now. He'd learned from Lilly that relationships had consequences. It wasn't a lesson he could quickly forget.

He lifted his lips, and his body protested with every inch he put between the two of them, a deep ache settling in his groin.

"I want you, Katie. You know that, don't you?" he asked her as she blinked up at him, her eyes languorous and her lips swollen and even redder now from his kisses.

"Yes, I think that's pretty evident," she said as she rocked herself against the hard length of him, sending a jolt of desire through his body that was almost his undoing.

From the gleam in her eyes, he had no doubt that she knew she wasn't playing fair, but two could play that game.

He stroked her pebbled nipples and she arched into his hands. A sweet pain shot through him as he hardened even more. Only then did he realize his mistake. His control was slipping away from him again and he wasn't sure that he even cared.

"You're still not sure, are you?" Katie licked her lips before letting out an exaggerated sigh.

He didn't dare move. One more squirm of her tight bottom against him and no matter what his misgivings, there would be no going back.

"I should be angry, but I understand. We barely know each other and then I bare my soul to you. You have to worry that I'm dragging you into my life, which is absurdly complicated right now."

"Is that really what you think? That because you are struggling right now I don't want to become involved? That's BS and you have to know it."

"So it's not me, it's you?" she asked. She stood and stepped away from him.

He felt her withdrawal as if some part of him were being ripped away. But much like the need to tear off a bandage and get the pain over with, this was for the best.

He stood and took a step toward her even though he knew he needed to walk away. This was madness. "I explained my reasons for us not getting involved. You have a life in New York that you will be going back to soon. Before Violet, we might have been able to make this work. A summer fling between two adults, yeah maybe. But I have more than my own needs to consider now."

He saw the moment she accepted his reasoning as all the defensiveness seemed to leave her body and she wrapped her arms around herself.

"I'm sorry. You've been nothing but kind to me. I don't know what's wrong with me. I'm not like this, you know. I don't go around throwing myself at men in New York."

Her words filled him with a surprising pleasure. He'd never believed that she reacted to other men the same way as to him, but it was good to hear it. But why was that? What made him different from all the men in New York?

Maybe that was the appeal. He wasn't the smart-dressed city boy that she was used to. He was just a simple beach bum, more comfortable in a pair of flip-flops than a pair of Gucci lace-ups.

Or was it the very thing that kept him holding her at arm's length? Was she just interested in him because she could walk away in a few weeks and never have to look back?

His heart told him that she was sincere in her interest in him, but his mind wasn't going to let him forget the way Lilly had walked away from him without ever looking back.

"It's late and you couldn't have gotten

much sleep today before Violet came home from school. Maybe it's best if we discuss this later when our minds are clearer," he said.

A sadness had filled Katie's eyes when she turned toward him. Or was it acceptance? "Good night, Katie."

"Good night, Dylan. Sleep well," she said as she headed for the doors leading back into the house.

He had no doubt that she knew there would be very little sleep for him tonight, just like he was certain she would be the reason.

CHAPTER SEVEN

"Hi, Daddy," Katie said when she heard the sound of her daddy's voice, gruff and comforting on her phone. She really should have called him earlier. She had no excuse to give him, but knowing her father there wouldn't be a need. Being a police officer in the NYPD had worn all the sensitivity out of him years ago.

"Katie dear, how are you? Have you gotten that Key West crew into shape yet?"

No, but they certainly were helping her get into shape. Or at least the experience there was helping her learn to deal with her problems. After all, she'd run as far south as she could. She'd given herself no option but to stop and deal with them.

Not that she could tell him that. That was the problem with a lie. You either had to continue the lie and live with the results, or you had to come clean about the lie you'd told which was always painful. She'd told her father that she was fine. How did she tell him now that she was struggling with anxiety and fear whenever something triggered memories of the shooting?

Her counselor advised her to be honest with her family so she could begin healing. But the thought of disappointing her father was more than she could handle now.

Baby steps. She needed to take baby steps right now. She only felt safe sharing those deepest memories haunting her with Dylan. And she hadn't even shared how empty she discovered her life was after the shooting. How could she, without him thinking that she wanted even more from him than their friendship?

"I'm actually learning a lot here. It's so much different from New York."

"How's that?" her father asked.

"Well, there's the weather. It's extremely humid and it rains a lot, but there are all these blooming trees and bushes. And there are these crazy iguanas. There was this huge one that came up on my back deck last night while I was sitting there. It was at least three feet long and it had these sharp teeth and these long spines on its back. It scared me to death."

"Did you shoot it?" her father asked.

"No, of course not. Dylan put it back in his garden." She knew her mistake the moment the words were out of her mouth. But it was too late. Her father had years of investigating under his belt. He never missed a thing.

"And who is this Dylan?" Her father's voice all business now. Captain John McGee Sr. alert and on duty.

"He's one of the flight crew members and he's my landlord." And the only man she'd ever met that could set her on fire with one touch. The night before had proven that. It also proved that Dylan was just as affected by her as she was by him.

She smiled, thinking of the way she had tortured him the night before. It was his own fault. Or was it? Dylan had told her more than once now that he didn't get involved in short-term relationships.

Her smile turned into a frown. She needed to accept that there could be nothing between the two of them. It wasn't fair to him to expect more.

Still, he'd been the one to pull her into his lap. That showed he was interested in her, even if it was just for a short time, right? But that was something he would ever admit to. Violet's mother had hurt him too deeply for him to trust anyone.

"Katie?" her father asked, "You still there?"

"Oh, sorry. Did I lose you?" she asked, wondering if her phone service was the problem or simply her mind so caught up in her thoughts of Dylan that she hadn't heard her father. It felt like her mind did a lot of wandering lately. "What were you saying?"

"I was saying that you need to remember that you are in Key West to do a job. I've told you about the dangers of getting romantically involved with your coworkers. Never ends well, Katie dear."

"Never?" she asked, teasing her father, who had been seeing a woman, Ms. Elizabeth from dispatch, since Katie was a teenager.

"I'm not joking. You've had a hard year. The last thing you need is to come back here with some heartache over one of them beach boys down there."

Her father had no idea just how hard the last months had been on her, but he was right. She didn't need to lose her heart to Dylan.

"It's not like that, Daddy. Don't you have enough to worry about with my brothers right now? You know I can take care of myself," she said, hoping this wasn't just another lie she was telling the two of them.

"I don't doubt that a bit, Katie dear, but..."

Her hands tightened on her phone as her father hesitated. This was what she had feared. As always the man somehow knew there was something she was hiding. It was a gift that made him a good detective.

"I know it's been hard on you, not having a mother to talk to you while you were growing up. But you know I'm always here if you need me, right?"

Her big strong father sounded so vulnerable that tears flooded her eyes. She wiped them with her free hand. She'd cried more in the last few months than she'd cried her whole life. "I know, Daddy. It's been good for me here. Really good."

"I'm glad to hear that," her father said,

sounding more like the man in charge that she was used to.

By the time she hung up with her father she'd somehow managed to reassure him that things were going to be okay and that soon she'd be on her way home to New York, ready to get back to her life in the big city, flying wherever she was needed and helping to save lives. Now all she had to do was to convince herself.

It had been a week of doing nothing but transfers that had Katie seeing red. Dylan had asked her to take some twelve-hour shifts working days and since she was the new person and only temporary she had agreed. She hadn't known the motive behind his request. She hadn't shared her experiences getting shot or the problems she was still learning to deal with just so Dylan could take her off the trauma calls. She'd assumed he understood what she needed was to get out there and function as a full-fledged flight nurse. Why couldn't he see that she needed to be treated like everyone else?

Or did he think, after hearing her story, that she couldn't do her job? There was only one way to handle this. She would have this out with him face-to-face as she'd been brought up to do.

A twinge of guilt hit her with the memory of the way she'd brushed off her father's concerns earlier in the week instead of facing her troubles. But this wasn't her father. This was business. This was her job. The one she was ready to fight for if it was necessary.

She knocked on the office door where she'd seen Dylan headed after the crew finished their last transfer from the Key West hospital to Miami. It had been an easy flight. They'd all been easy flights the last three shifts. She'd ended up the third wheel on the crew and been forced to take all the transfers. It wasn't that she minded helping out. It was the fact that she wasn't being trusted with the other calls.

Except for work, she and Dylan had rarely seen each other. She didn't need a flashing neon sign to tell her why he was keeping his distance. He'd been very plain that he wasn't interested in becoming involved with her. It hurt. She'd have to admit that, but she understood his reasons. She couldn't undo a past that had caused him to shy from short-term relationships and hurting Violet was the last thing she wanted. The little girl had quickly taken residence in Katie's heart and she knew that it wasn't going to be easy to leave her when the time came to return to New York. Confusing Dylan's daughter with a relationship that had no future wouldn't be fair.

She could hear that he was on a phone call and had turned to leave when the office door opened.

"Hey. Sorry I had a call I needed to take. What's up?" Dylan said. His eyes looked tired and his hair was once more rumpled as if his hands had pulled at it too long.

"Is something wrong?" she asked, watching him closely. If he'd been speaking to the NYC office he would tell her, wouldn't he?

"Nothing for you to worry about," he said.

"What does that mean?" Had he told the New York office about the anxiety she was dealing with? The fact that she was suffering from what could only be PTSD? Had they decided to offer her another one of those desk jobs that she had already turned down after the shooting? Or were they working together to get her off the regular flight crew and only allow her to do transfers, just like he was doing here? Was that the plan? That once she returned to New York she'd be shuffled into some position where she'd transfer patients from one hospital to the other, never getting to see what was really going on in the city? Never getting to do the job of saving lives that she had been trained to do?

"It's nothing. Just some changes that are coming. I wish Alex was here to deal with it all," Dylan said. "Would you like something to drink? I really need a water."

Moving back, she watched as he walked down the hall to the kitchen. He came back with two bottles of water and handed her one of them. Sitting down at the desk, she glanced at the piece of paper in front of him where someone had been doodling stick figures. Was that a crown sitting on one of their heads?

It was plain to see that he wasn't going to tell her who he'd been talking to. She decided on the up-front method of interrogation that her father had taught her.

"Was it the New York office? Are they going to fire me? Is that why I haven't been on the trauma calls?"

There was no way to tell if the surprise in

Dylan's eyes was due to her discovering the truth or her being way off the mark.

"Why would they fire you?" Dylan asked. He took a deep breath and then motioned to the chair.

"Because you told them I couldn't do my job. Isn't that why you only have me doing the transfers? Because you don't trust me?" she asked. She felt all the fight leave her as she voiced her greatest fear. By opening up to Dylan she had laid herself open for this, but she'd thought she could trust him to understand that she would never let her own problems affect her job or the safety of her patients. Had she been wrong?

"Maybe you should start from the beginning because nothing you've said since you walked into this room makes sense."

"Neither does anything you've said. You're holding something back and if it isn't that I'm going to get fired, what is it?" For a moment she thought he was going to tell her what had upset him so much, but then he shook his head.

"It's nothing to do with you. *That* I can tell you. And as far as you taking the transfers, that's a lot of what we do. As the fill-in you've ended up with a lot of those calls because the regular team has been busy during the night and I thought you could give them a break," he explained. "And if I have a problem with any of the staff that would require me to discipline or change their duties I would talk to them. You can trust me, Katie. I thought you knew that."

Their radios went off and they both stood. "Stat STEMI transfer to Miami," Katie read as she headed out to the hall to join the rest of the crew. Doors opened up down the hall and they both met the crew.

"I've got this one," Dylan said to Max as he was zipping up his flight suit. She turned, surprised to see that Dylan had grabbed his own suit. They were buckled in their seats and in the air in less than four minutes.

"What brings you out of the office, boss? Getting bored?" Jackie asked.

"I just needed some flight time. You know how it is. And how many times do I need to tell you not to call me 'boss.' Alex is still the boss here," Dylan said, his voice over the headsets carried an edge she hadn't heard before.

They worked quietly together as she prepared the IV fluids and he readied the monitors they would need to transport someone who was having an acute heart attack.

"Don't they have a cath lab at the hospital?" she asked. She was pretty sure she had seen that they did some cardiac procedures.

"Only for diagnostic testing. The cardiologist in Miami must have determined that this guy needed immediate intervention," Dylan said.

Landing at the hospital, she was glad to see that the nurses on duty had their patient ready to go with an IV line running in each forearm.

"What's the story?" she asked as she switched the man's oxygen tubing over to their portable tank while Dylan transferred him over to their portable monitors.

"Here's the twelve lead," a nurse said as she handed Katie a copy of an EKG, which showed a textbook-perfect elevation of the man's ST segment.

"Mr. Singh, I'm Katie, a flight nurse with Heli-Care. We're going to take a fast trip up north to Miami where there's a cardiologist who can take care of your heart. Is that okay with you?"

The man nodded his head and they finished packing him up. They left the hospital with his family standing at the entrance waving their goodbyes. It was only when their headsets were on and the skids had left the grown that Katie exchanged a look with Dylan.

"I don't like the way this guy looks," she said, turning her head away from the patient. The dusky blue of the man's lips told her there was not a lot of time before he would be in trouble.

"I'm increasing his oxygen," Dylan said as he switched the oxygen tubing from the portable tank to the oxygen inside the cab. "I've got him up to fifteen liters. Do you see any change?"

"SaO2 is eighty-eight, respirations shallow at thirty. BP is falling too…eighty-eight over fifty-three," she responded. "I'm opening up the fluids to see if it will help with the hypotension. And I'm going to prepare for intubation."

"I'm radioing ahead. They need to be ready to take this guy straight into the cath lab." As Dylan started the process with dispatch to get in touch with the receiving hospital, she did a quick neuro check, noticing that the patient was harder to arouse. "Hey, Dylan. He's less responsive. It might be the morphine they gave him, but it's a definite change. I'm going to go ahead and intubate."

"Do it. This guy is going bad fast. I'm worried about that blood pressure too," Dylan said as he pushed the button on the monitor to recycle. The new reading wasn't any better than the earlier one.

"Interior wall ST elevation? Cardiogenic shock?" she asked as she pushed the medications she had drawn up for intubation. His head on the stretcher resting between her knees, she positioned the man's head and slid the laryngoscope in place, visualized the vocal cords and inserted the endotracheal tube. With the Ambu bag connected, she started ventilating the patient as Dylan leaned over and checked for placement.

"Good breath sounds. I'm waiting for an order from the doctor for a vasopressor. I wouldn't have this problem if Alex was here. I'd have an order by now," Dylan said.

She had so many questions concerning Alex's location and when he'd be returning. But they'd have to wait until they weren't fifteen hundred feet in the air.

"Going in for final approach," Jackie said through the headsets.

"Thank goodness," Katie said. "I want to hand over this guy before he deteriorates anymore."

"See, not all transfers are boring," Dylan said as the skids touched the ground. They hit the ground running as soon as the stretcher was unloaded.

Katie had thought that she would have a chance to talk to Dylan when they arrived back at the hangar, but she was quickly sent off on another flight with Max. And while her grumpy coworker was growing on her, she missed having Dylan by her side.

And that was a problem, wasn't it? She'd be leaving in a few weeks. There'd be no more flights with Dylan. No more crab boils or late-night talks. And no more kisses that set her body on fire with a longing that she had never felt before.

But she hadn't come here for a temporary hookup. She'd come here to heal and she knew that she was making progress.

She was just now accepting that some

parts of her life had changed forever. Seeing that the changes could be dealt with, that she could learn ways to deal with the anxiety when it was triggered, was a good start.

She'd do her job and when her time was over here she would be ready to return to her real life, her life in New York where her family was waiting for her.

That was what she needed to concentrate on instead of some kisses that she'd shared with a man that could never be hers.

CHAPTER EIGHT

DYLAN WASN'T SURE what drove him to Katie's door. Maybe it was the pacing he'd been doing back and forth in his bedroom while remembering the way Katie had felt in his arms, so soft and warm. Maybe it was his cold and lonely bed that made him question all his cautious rules meant to protect him and his daughter?

With Violet at a sleepover, he'd had the whole night to himself. But the light coming from Katie's cottage had kept him from settling down. Knowing she was awake, like him, was having the same effect as if he'd drank a whole pot of coffee by himself.

He'd opened a book, read a few words and shut it. He'd turned on the sports channel and turned it off.

What was she doing over there? Was she

thinking of him like he was thinking of her? Was she reliving the kiss they'd shared like he was?

Or was it her worry for her job that was keeping her up tonight? Their conversation had been interrupted by dispatch earlier that day. It wouldn't be right to let her continue to question her place on the flight team without him reassuring her that she was wanted and needed there.

He needed to convince her that he had total faith in her abilities. He couldn't understand why she worried about her future with Heli-Care. He'd worked with her enough now to know that she was much more than a capable flight nurse. And her employee file had been filled with excellent reviews.

He knocked on the door and waited. And waited. Had she fallen asleep with all the lights on? He started to leave.

"Dylan, what are you doing here?" Katie asked as she opened the door. While she wasn't in the tank top and shorts he'd been fantasizing about on his walk to her cottage, the long white T-shirt that barely covered the top of her thighs was enough to create new fantasies that would definitely be keeping him up again that night.

"You busy?" he asked. "We were interrupted this afternoon so I thought maybe we could talk."

His excuse for seeing her sounded weak even to his own ears. Their conversation could have waited until the next day. But his need to see her, to talk to her and, yes, the hope of more kisses like they'd shared before, wouldn't wait.

"Okay. Come on in. Is Violet asleep?" Katie said, though she didn't sound as if she was as excited about seeing him as he was to see her. Instead she appeared distracted.

"No, I'm on my own tonight. She's spending the night with a friend."

"I was just finishing up my paintings," she said as she led the way through the cottage to the small open living room where he could see an easel had been set on the dining room tabletop.

He walked around where he could see a canvas watercolor painting of a white heron. He recognized the setting as the one from her back deck. Picking up the canvas, he studied the details of the large bird. Its head was cocked up and its eyes, piercing, seemed to stare out at him. This wasn't the work of a hobbyist.

"You're good. Real good. Did you ever consider going into art in college?" he asked.

"And give my dad a heart attack? No, that was one profession I never considered." She said as she moved around the room putting her supplies away.

"So what were some of the professions you considered?" he asked, leaning back against the island that separated the room from the kitchen.

"Well, when I first got out of high school I considered following my other family members into the NYPD, but I've always liked the sciences. Especially my anatomy and physiology classes. They were my favorite. I thought about medical school, but I didn't feel that I had the patience I'd need to commit to that many years of school. A nursing degree gave me so many options. What about you? What made you decide to become a paramedic?"

"I'd had a lot of jobs since high school. Most were things I learned working with my dad growing up on the marina. A little construction work, some boat engine work, lots of general handyman jobs. But it was when I heard the community was in need of more first responders that I decided to look into becoming a paramedic. It was quite an adventure and I loved every minute of it. I wouldn't want to do anything else."

"That's why you get it. Get me. Isn't it? You understand how I feel about my job. It's my life," Katie said as she took a step closer to him.

"I can't pretend to understand what you've been going through. Being shot while just trying to do your job? That's a deep betrayal after everything you've done to help others. But yes, I understand the fear of not being able to do the job you feel you were born to do." He started to make a move toward her. He only needed to touch her.

She took a step back confusing him. Hadn't he just read that same need in her own eyes? Or was it just his imagination?

"Want something to eat?" Katie turned her back to him as she opened the refrigerator. "Or drink?"

He placed the canvas back on the table,

then saw that there was another one that had been laid beside it.

There was no Florida sunshine or bright colored blooms in this one. Where the other painting had been light and cheerful, this one was dark and menacing with the only light coming from a few lit buildings in the dark background. A street of dark blues and browns was empty and lonely.

It was hard to believe the same artist could have painted them both.

Moving away from the table, he took a seat in a side chair as Katie shut the refrigerator door without taking anything out. Was his presence troubling her? If she needed space, he would give it to her. He'd say his piece and then leave.

He waited until she took a chair across from him. "I'm sorry about this. Interrupting you. I shouldn't have come over this late. I just saw your light on and thought..."

"That I was here worrying about if that phone call that upset you had something to do with my job?" Katie said, interrupting him. "I could have been. But no. I decided that I needed a little art therapy so I got my paints out."

"Art therapy?" That explained the picture so full of darkness. "Is that like the shopping therapy Jo and Summer are always talking about going to Miami for?"

"For me? Yeah. I guess painting has always been an escape for me. It's kind of like what some people get from reading. Or shopping, I guess. My counselor recommended it in New York, but I couldn't bring myself to pick up a pencil or brush then. Seeing that heron seemed to awaken that part of me again," Katie said as she moved to the edge of her seat.

"I'm glad. If you'd like, I can see about getting Pascal over here to pose for you?" he joked, trying to lighten the mood.

"I think I'll stick to birds, thank you," Katie said, a smile playing around the corners of her lips before disappearing.

"Why are you really here, Dylan?" she asked.

"I couldn't stay away," he said with an honesty that surprised himself. Unable to take his eyes from hers, he reached out a hand to her. She looked down at it then placed her hand in his. But there was a hesitation that hadn't been there before and he couldn't ignore it. "What's wrong, Katie?"

"Besides the fact that my whole life is a tangled mess and I'm wondering if I'm about to get myself even more tangled up in a relationship that we've both admitted has no future? Nothing has changed, Dylan. In a few weeks I'll be returning to New York."

Her words made him draw his hand back, but then her fingers tightened their grip on his, as if it was a lifeline, confusing him even more. He didn't want to complicate Katie's life.

"I'm as confused as you. I'm not into holiday flings or one-night stands. But this… whatever it is between us, I don't feel in control of where it's leading us," he said as he stood and pulled her into his arms. "Tell me to leave and I will."

"I don't want you to leave. I want you. But I know you have your own rules about who you get involved with. And I don't want you to regret this. We both have to understand that this need that keeps drawing us together, it's just a temporary thing." She bit down on her bottom lip. "Can we do this? Have this time together without any expectations? Go into this with the understanding that neither one of us will let this complicate things between us. People do that all the time, right?"

People might, but he didn't. He had never had a taste for one-night stands. It was why he had stipulations that he didn't get involved with someone who wasn't a local. And even that had been off the table since Violet had come into his life.

He'd been honest with Katie about everything, from her job to his history with Lilly and how that had affected him. But could he share his fear that it might be too late for him to keep things uncomplicated between them? Because the way he was beginning to feel about Katie was already complicated. Taking her as his lover would make their parting even more difficult. He was risking the pain he'd felt when Lilly left him.

But wasn't Katie worth the risk? Wasn't spending this time together worth it? As long as he could keep Violet protected, he could handle everything else.

He brushed his hand over her soft cheek and lifted her chin up toward his face. Emerald-green eyes met his own with questions he wasn't capable of answering. They were both stepping into the unknown, but they were doing it together.

She was close enough that he could see a sprinkle of freckles across her nose he'd noticed for the first time. His lips brushed over them then grazed her mouth. He held his breath, waiting to see if she thought him worth the risk as well. When her lips parted, he rushed inside with an eagerness that he had never felt before. It was if she had thrown him an unexpected lifeline that was the only hope he had to survive. Their kiss was more passion than finesse as their need for each other took control.

How they made it to her bedroom he would never know.

Her arms wrapped around him and he lifted her off her feet. He walked them to the bed without breaking their kiss, unwilling to take a chance that one of them might come to their senses.

His shirt hit the bedroom floor minus most of its buttons. Her T-shirt quickly followed. He was finding it hard to remove the tiny polka-dot shorts she wore with her hand inside his shorts.

Her shorts and panties slid to the ground

where they joined the rest of her clothes as her hand circled him. His gasp broke their kiss and they both came up for a breath of air.

"Do you have a condom?" Katie asked as she ran her hand up the length of his shaft.

Her words broke through the fog of desire that had taken over. How had he forgotten about needing a condom? It was his responsibility to keep her safe.

"I've got it." He stepped away from her and reached into his back pocket before discarding his shorts. Fumbling with his wallet, he pulled out the foil wrapper. He forced his lungs to take a deep breath and willed his body to relax. His control was slipping and he hadn't even touched her beautiful bare body.

One look at her lying on the bed and his body went right back into overdrive. He'd never been so affected by a woman. Not even Lilly, who he'd thought he loved. He forced thoughts of his ex and of love out of his mind. This was not the time or place for either.

He crawled onto the bed and covered her. "Katie, you are so beautiful."

The sensual feel of her breasts against his

own skin set his pulse racing and he covered her perfect breast with his hand. Her heart beat against his palm in a fast rhythm that matched his own. Her nipple peaked against his hand.

"I want to know all of you. I want to kiss every intimate inch of you. But where do I start?" His lips trailed down her neck and she shivered against him. "Should I start here?"

"Or maybe here?" His lips replaced his hand on her breast. The feel of her tight nipple against his tongue set him on fire. His hand moved down her body and parted her curls. She was warm and wet against his fingers.

His lips followed a path down her abdomen, her stomach muscles quivering beneath his mouth. Her body arched up from the bed as his fingers found that sweet spot of her clit.

"Dylan, I can't…" Katie said, her breaths coming fast.

"Can't? But you're too strong of a woman to give up when it's something you want. I know that. Do you want this, Katie?" His lips skimmed down her thighs.

"Oh, yes. I want it." Her breaths were

ragged as she spoke. She moaned as she arched her body up to meet his mouth.

He pleasured her with his tongue and fingers. Her body tensed against his as her climax tore through her.

Katie came the way she did everything else: strong and fierce. Her scream cut through the room. It wasn't enough for him. He wanted to hear it again and again as she came for him. But his own breathing told him he couldn't take the torture of holding himself back much longer.

"Dylan, please. I want more," Katie gasped, her eyes bright with tears. Of course she would. She always fought for what she wanted. She'd always want more.

"I'll give you everything I have, sweet Katie," he murmured, brushing back strands of silky hair from her face.

With the condom safely in place, he entered her with one thrust. The warmth of her surrounded him, taking him inside her as her body opened up to him, stretched his control to a dangerous level. But still he held on. He'd promised her everything and he would give it to her.

The woman that thought she had lost a

part of herself in New York was not the same woman in this bedroom. Wrapping her legs around him, she met each thrust with a demand that brought him deeper. Her body tensed and shuddered against him. He let himself follow her into the climax that took control of them both as they reached a summit higher than he'd ever climbed before.

Later, as he curled his body around hers, he knew what he had experienced with Katie was something more than he had ever experienced before.

With a response time that came from years of being awakened by emergency calls from dispatch, her phone only rang once before Katie was out of bed and grabbing it from the floor where it had landed the night before. Seeing her oldest brother's number on the display was surprising. She'd done her weekly required check-in with him only the day before. Why would he be calling her now? A familiar chill, one that came from being in a family of police officers, froze her in place.

As Dylan rolled over and sat up, she hit

the button while she pulled her T-shirt over her head. "What's wrong?"

"Something wrong with me calling my baby sister? You still enjoying that hellish heat down there?" a deep voice asked on the other line.

"Wrong? No. Unexpected? Yes." She knew her brothers too well. There was a reason for this call. Her brother wasn't calling her to ask about the weather. "What's up, Junior?"

"We've got him, sis," her brother said.

She didn't have to ask who he was talking about. She'd known, even though they'd kept it from her as much as possible, that her father and two oldest brothers were on a mission to arrest the person responsible for hurting her.

For her part, she'd tried to forget that there was someone out there on the loose who'd almost ended her life. It wasn't like they'd picked her out specifically. She'd just been in the wrong place at the wrong time. She had no reason to fear that he was going to come back to finish her off like he had her patient.

Or had that been her fear? Was that why she couldn't stand to have someone at her back? Was that the reason she was afraid in crowds? Her counselor had suggested this to her, but she'd always denied that she was still afraid of the shooter. Maybe she'd been wrong.

"You're sure it's him?" she asked as she looked over to where Dylan now sat up in her bed. He brushed back the sandy curls that had fallen into his eyes and a fire stirred inside her. How could just a look from this man affect her this way?

She didn't want to talk about the guy who'd shot her. She wanted to climb back in bed with Dylan and forget all about that night.

But that would be selfish and unappreciative. Her family had worked hard to make sure this guy got caught when her case could have joined the file room of cold cases.

"We found a good informant. It seems our shooter is a bragger. It's him." Which meant her brothers and probably her father had been laying out money to catch the guy.

"So what happens now?" she asked. A sheet was wrapped around her along with a pair of muscled arms. She hadn't even realized she was shivering.

"They picked him up last night after the

warrant was issued. He's got a record, so hopefully the judge won't let him out on bond."

His words sent a rush of anger washing through her. After all the hard work her family as well as the other officers involved had done, the guy could still walk free? After all the pain he had caused in her life? After he'd taken the life of a young man?

"No," she said. "They can't do that. It's not right. He killed someone. He could have killed me."

And he changed my life forever. She was just beginning to accept that. Through her counseling sessions she'd been forced to face that she would never be the same Katie Lee McGee she had been before. Now she might have to live with the knowledge that the man responsible could be out there living his life like nothing ever happened.

"The district attorney is pushing to hold him without bail. He had a gun in his possession when they found him. If it matches the bullets we got from the deceased and... Well, if they match we'll have a more solid case." Her brother skipped over the words *the bullet that they dug out of you*, but she knew what he was trying not to say and she still felt the sting of the words. Acknowledging that she had been shot was hard for her and he knew it. "But, Katie, you know how these things work. There's no guarantee that the judge will agree with the DA."

Another shiver hit her and Dylan's arms tightened even more. Leaning back, she rested her head against him. She was suddenly so tired.

"I know," she said wearily as all the anger drained from her. She'd grown up with table talk of suspects that had been released as soon as they were brought in. "It's okay, Junior. I know it's not your fault. I appreciate everything you and the rest of the investigators have done. Make sure they know that, okay."

She hung up the phone not sure how she should feel. Would it really be worse if the person responsible for shooting her got off than if he'd never been found?

The warmth of Dylan's body behind her was a comfort she hadn't known she needed. But she did need him. She needed him now. Turning in his arms, she proceeded to show him just how much.

CHAPTER NINE

DYLAN WATCHED VIOLET and Katie talk colors and textures as they made their way through the art store. When Katie had mentioned she needed some supplies, Violet had been quick to volunteer to show her around the local hobby shops.

"Can I get some paints too?" Violet asked him. "I'll be careful with them."

He could see the carpet in her room covered in spilt containers of paint. His daughter had a love of color and art, which Katie had been encouraging over the last week.

They'd gotten into a routine of spending the warm evenings when neither was working on either his or her deck. While he grilled their supper, Katie taught Violet some of the basics of using watercolors. Though they were being careful of their interactions when

Violet was present, they always managed a few clandestine kisses good-night. Still, he couldn't help but worry about his daughter as he saw the two of them become closer. He'd made a point of reminding Violet that Katie was only here temporarily like the other renters they'd had over the summer.

"She'll only use them with me on the deck," Katie said.

Two sets of eyes from the two most beautiful girls in the world stared up with him. It was official. He was outnumbered.

"Okay, as long as Violet understands the rules. She has a tendency to ignore the rules she doesn't agree with," he said, giving his daughter a look that had her giggling instead of chastised.

A part of him winced at his words. He felt like a hyprocrite. He had been breaking his most important rule since the night he'd slept with Katie.

But he had no regrets. Watching Katie and Violet with their heads bent together over a display of brushes, though, he felt his concern for his daughter intensify. He was an adult, and both he and Katie had gone into their new relationship knowing that it was only temporary.

But Violet was only eight. Providing stability had been his first and most important priority. He'd been careful to make sure that his daughter knew he wasn't going anywhere. He'd always be there for her.

But Katie wouldn't be. Hopefully his daughter would understand when her new friend had to leave.

"Can we walk down to that place with the funny art?" Violet asked after they'd paid for their purchases. "The place with the big statue of that bull dog?"

"Sure, but I don't think this is exactly what Katie is used to." There were a lot of artists that sold their work in the local shops. Pictures and paintings of everything from roosters to pirates hung in the gift shops and galleries. It was definitely not the same as the artwork available for viewing at the Metropolitan Museum of Art in New York City.

"It sounds like fun to me," Katie said. "This is a part of Key West I haven't seen."

They followed the sidewalk and turned onto Duval. A favorite with tourist for the local shops, it was more crowded than the other streets.

The crowd. He hadn't given a thought to how Katie might react to the tourist-packed streets.

"We don't want to get separated," he said as he took Violet's and Katie's hands.

"I'm not a baby," Violet grumbled, but she didn't pull away from him.

Katie squeezed his hand, but there wasn't any other sign that the people surrounding her were creating the anxiety he'd seen in her face before. Could it be that she was finally recovering?

They played tourists as they stopped in the brightly displayed shops. Katie bought an oil painting in a store that specialized in estate sails, before following Violet into an ice cream shop with fanciful creations.

As he and Katie ate their creamy dessert, Violet chased a small rooster around the table while eating a rainbow-colored ice cream cone.

"Having fun?" he asked, not knowing how to ask if the crowds were a problem for her. "We can leave if you need to."

"I'm fine. More than fine," she said. The

smile on her face was genuine. “Thanks for inviting me.”

“Thank you for helping Violet with the art lessons. She’s always had an artistic flair but I hadn’t thought she was old enough to take lessons.”

“All I’m showing her is the basics. I’m sure you can find a professional to teach her when I leave,” she said before looking away.

He glanced over to where Violet was talking to the rooster she’d cornered, to make sure they had some privacy, then placed his hand under her chin. Turning her face up to his, he stared down into troubled green eyes.

“It’s okay, Katie. We both know our time together is short-lived. We probably should start getting Violet used to the idea, though. You’re her new best friend and I’m not sure she understands that you are only here temporarily, though I’ve told her that your home is in New York.”

His hand brushed over her cheek then trailed down her face. She had an expressive face with its bright eyes and big smile. He’d taken to storing memories of these times they shared.

He knew how her eyes sparkled when Violet told her a joke. How her lips turned up into the perfect smile every time she saw him. There was no shyness, no awkward moments between the two of them. And then there were the memories of their lovemaking. He'd never had a lover that was so responsive and passionate. He could see that she was returning to the happy, funny woman that Alex had once described to him.

Over half of her time in Key West had passed and she hadn't displayed any issues on a flight since the gunshot-wound patient they'd picked up on the beach the first week she'd arrived. Even Max had come to accept her place in their crew, something that seemed to surprise the staff as much as it had surprised her.

She was healing and he was thankful for that.

They toured a few more art galleries before calling it a day. It was a memorable day for all of them. While Violet exclaimed over her new paints, Katie clutched the framed portrait of one of Key West's famous roosters as if she had a priceless piece of art.

When Violet commented that he hadn't bought anything for himself, he didn't bother to tell her that he'd been given the best gift of all. He'd spent a perfect day with his two favorite people. What more could he ask for?

Katie couldn't say exactly when the change had taken place. One morning she had woken up feeling like she would never be the person she'd been before the shooting and the next morning she hadn't felt quite as broken. Slowly each day, she'd seen a change as she worked to fit in with the Key West crew. As she learned more about what it took for her to cope with the triggers to her anxiety, she grew in confidence. As she grew in confidence, her spirits lifted and the next day was a little bit better.

Now she woke up with a smile on her face, looking forward to the day. She refused to acknowledge that a big part of why she felt better was because of the nights she was spending with Dylan when Violet was away with a friend or a grandparent.

And it wasn't just the nights. They were spending every minute they could spare together now as her time in Key West ran out. There wasn't a night off that she didn't spend with Dylan and Violet. And if Dylan happened to work a shift when she was off, Katie had begun having Violet for sleepovers. On those nights, after Dylan had called to wish his daughter a good night, the two of them would spend hours talking. But she knew things couldn't go on like this. She needed to start making plans to return to New York. She needed to start preparing Violet for her departure. She and Dylan had never let the little girl see that they were more than friends. But the amount of time they spent together could confuse Violet, even though the she and Dylan talked openly about her home in New York where she would be returning.

But like everything else that she couldn't deal with, she pushed her thoughts of leaving Dylan away. Her life was improving each day. She just needed a little more time here. She'd thought about asking for an extension on her contract in Key West, especially since Alex was still out, but she knew that wasn't the answer. No matter when she left Key West it was going to be hard. Staying longer would just make it worse.

And it wasn't just Dylan and Violet she was going to miss. She felt like one of the crew now. She'd worked with each one of them enough now that she thought they felt comfortable with her. She hoped they each felt as if they could count on her as a dependable partner.

She'd even learned how to deal with Max. When he'd given her crap on a flight to a car-bicycle accident, telling her not to run off all the first responders, she'd been ready. Telling him to make sure he didn't puke on their patient had gotten a rare laugh from the man. Since that day, he hadn't given her any trouble.

But her favorite partner was still Dylan. They worked together with a familiarity that would normally take years to perfect.

As they flew over the island together on their way to a possible drowning, her confidence was at an all-time high. She had a lot of experience in drowning calls in New York. Early resuscitation was always the key.

"Heli-Care Key West, be advised we have an update," the dispatcher called over their headsets.

"Go ahead," Dylan answered.

"The original call has been updated with two, not one, two drowning victims with one victim still not accounted for," the dispatcher said. "Key West Fire and Rescue is on site with your landing zone info."

Jackie signed off and changed their radio channel. Receiving their landing zone coordinates, she made a pass over the area of beach giving them a view of the EMTs who were working the scene.

"Two adults. It looked like one of them is doing okay," she said as she pointed to where a woman sat holding a small child with a rescuer applying an oxygen mask.

"Or there's another victim we're not seeing. Let's get down there where we can help, Jackie," Dylan said. "Maybe we'll be lucky and this will be just a trip to the beach."

The fire department had positioned their landing zone farther down the beach where they had cleared all the beachgoers from the area, which made the trip back to the scene a short hike.

The resistance of the sand as they fought their way to the scene had the two of them breathing heavily by the time they got to the first victim. She was a woman in her midthirties, not much older than Katie, who sat holding a little boy no more than four in her arms, rocking him between her bouts of coughing. The young child clung to his mother but he didn't cry.

Katie noted that though she had a cough, her lips were pink. She would need to be taken to the emergency room and watched for pulmonary complications such as pneumonia, but she wouldn't be taking a flight with them.

Leaving the woman with the EMT, she followed Dylan to where first responders performed CPR on a young man.

"What's the story?" she asked as she took over compressions from a young woman who was beginning to tire.

"It seems that this couple's little boy wandered off and the two of them panicked and hit the water looking for him. They both got caught in the undertow. An onlooker got the woman out, but the husband went down before he could go back for him."

"What's the estimated downtime?" Dylan asked as he started opening their scene bag and applying monitor pads.

"The guy who brought him in says it was less than a minute. He's a firefighter from North Florida and he started CPR immediately," said the EMT who was using an

Ambu bag to ventilate the patient. "Total downtime is just at fifteen minutes."

"Time for a pulse check," the young EMT who she relieved said.

Katie placed her fingers against the man's neck and counted. The feel of blood pulsing through the man's carotid took her by surprise. "There's a pulse. We have a pulse."

She motioned to where the monitor that Dylan had just turned on showed a normal sinus rhythm.

"You sure?" asked the EMT who was preparing to continue chest compressions. "It could be a pulseless rate."

"Of course I'm sure." She wanted to take his challenge personally, but she remembered this was one of the crews she'd seen at her first MVC flight. She was going to have to live with the fallout from her loss of composure that day.

Checking behind her, the man placed his fingers where hers had been, then gave her a thumbs-up along with a big smile.

Maybe it wouldn't take as long as she thought to overcome that bad first impression she had given. Not that it really mattered. She'd be leaving soon and all those first responders that had seen her lose her cool that day wouldn't give her another thought.

"Katie, why don't you intubate this guy properly while I go talk to his wife," Dylan said before leaving them and walking over to where the woman continued to rock her little boy.

She bit her lip to keep from smiling. The EMT on scene had placed a temporary pre-hospital airway that could be inserted quickly, but most of the flight crew preferred to change over to an endotracheal tube before transporting if possible. Dylan was making a point to the EMT guy that he trusted his partner to intubate their patient.

She retrieved her supplies from the scene bag and replaced the temporary airway with the laryngoscope. She followed it with the endotracheal tube and quickly had the Ambu bag attached and began ventilating the patient.

The trip back to the helicopter where Jackie waited for them was a hard one. She was used to carrying people over hot asphalt, not hot sand where her feet sank down with every step. But she wasn't about to let the firefighters assisting them see her sweat. At least not figuratively. There was nothing she could do about the sweat that ran down her face into her flight suit.

As soon as they were buckled in and had lifted off, Katie got her Ambu bag changed over to the ventilator while Dylan called Miami for a consult with a trauma physician.

She did a neurological assessment and discovered that surprisingly the man's pupils were responsive. The percentage of people that survived a drowning was low, but it looked like this guy had a chance.

"Thanks for the vote of confidence back there," she told Dylan once their patient was settled.

"What vote? You don't need votes. There's nothing wrong with your confidence," Dylan replied.

"Thanks to you." She remembered that it wasn't just her and Dylan having a conversation, and added, "Working with this whole crew has been good for my confidence. You're all a great crew."

"Make sure you tell the big office guys in New York that when you get home," Jackie said over the headset. "They seem to think we play beach volleyball all day. Which reminds me, how are you at volleyball?"

"I haven't played since high school phys ed, why?" Katie asked as she did another neurological check on their patient.

"His pupils are still responsive. He might be one of the lucky few who survive. I wish he'd be a little more responsive, though," she said.

"He can be responsive after we land. The last thing we want is for him to wake up and start fighting us," Dylan said.

"I'm not a newbie. I've got my meds ready if he starts to come around. I'm not for fighting this guy either."

"Another few pounds and he would have been too heavy for us to fly. ETA in ten. Just make sure he stays out till then," Jackie said.

He was still unconscious when they left the emergency room, but the charge nurse promised she would let them know if he woke up on her shift.

They got a call from dispatch for transport from the hospital, but had to refuse it. A storm was moving in and the ceiling was too low for flying. They made it back to base as the storm broke, soaking them as they headed into their quarters.

The heavy rain was forecasted to last the night, but they made sure their scene bags and helicopter had been restocked while Jackie ran the necessary safety checks before they turned in for the night.

When her phone rang, she knew it would be Dylan. She kept her voice quiet so she wouldn't be overheard. "So what was that strange question of Jackie's about playing volleyball?"

"There's a volleyball tournament between all the first responders every year. There's an entrance fee for each player and the money goes to the winning team's charity. Jackie's our coach. Why, you want to play?"

"I've never played beach volleyball. I don't think I'd be much of an asset. Is your team any good?"

"We're awful. Besides, the firefighters have an unfair advantage. They have their tallest members on their team. Then there are the police. Most of those guys are in really good shape. We're a bunch of paramedics and nurses with a couple of retired military pilots. We haven't got a chance."

"Don't let Jackie hear you say that." She snuggled down into the sheets. Her eyes were getting heavy.

"Of course, we do have one defense that the others don't have." Dylan's voice was getting softer now. She knew that meant he was getting sleepy too. She only had to close her eyes to see that drowsy, sexy look he got right before he fell asleep. Not that they'd had many sleepovers. With Violet spending a couple nights a week away from home while he worked, he preferred to have her home with him at night.

"What's the defense?" she asked.

"Somehow every year the other team underestimates Jo and Summer. Then right when Jo is in the middle of charming them, Summer comes in for the kill. They never see it coming. At least not the first time," he said as he yawned.

"Sounds like fun. I'd like to come if I'm here." The finality of the words hit her. She only had three weeks before she would be leaving. Twenty-one days. After that life in Key West would go on without her.

"You know you're ready," Dylan said.

She didn't know how to take his words.

Was he in a hurry for her to go? No. She wouldn't believe that he wanted to rush her into leaving. "I'm glad you have a lot of confidence in me, but neither of us knows that."

"It's the confidence you have in yourself. You've got it back, Katie. I don't know if it's the counseling or just being away from New York. Maybe Alex was right and you just needed a change for a few weeks. You're not the same woman who walked into this office five weeks ago."

She wasn't. She had changed in ways she'd never imagined. And it hadn't all been from her counseling or from having a change in scenery. The biggest change had resulted from Dylan coaching her along the way. He'd called her out every time she'd tried to deny she had a problem. He'd told her what he expected of her and then told her that he knew she could do it. And that was even when he didn't know her.

What couldn't a woman do with a man like that backing her?

They said good-night with his words still echoing in her ears. Was she really ready to return to the tough streets of New York?

Could she return home and still have this new confidence? How would she ever know if she didn't try?

CHAPTER TEN

IT WAS A RARE DAY when all three of the women on their flight crew had the day off together, so they decided to celebrate with a trip to Miami. The fact that Jo and Summer had included Katie filled her with even more grief over the people she would be leaving behind soon. She didn't mention to any of her coworkers that there were just over two weeks until her time was up in Key West. She wanted to thank them all, but she felt it would be better if she waited until her last week to start saying her goodbyes. And today was for celebrating, not spending her time thinking about something she couldn't change. Dylan invited her out with him to downtown Key West for a night where the restaurants and shops stayed open late and the local artists displayed their art on the sidewalks and she hadn't brought anything that she felt would be suitable.

Katie hadn't left the islands by car since she'd arrived in Key West, so she had forgotten what a long trip it was when you weren't going by air.

"So, what's up with you and Dylan?" Summer asked as they sped up Highway 1 in Jo's Mustang convertible.

Katie had wondered how long it would take until the two women got around to questioning her about her and Dylan's relationship. They held out fifteen minutes more than she had bet Dylan they would that morning before they'd arrived to pick her up. Dylan believed the two women would start nosing their way into his and her relationship the minute the car door shut. He was wrong. They lasted almost thirty minutes.

Dylan had left it up to Katie to tell her friends whatever she felt comfortable with. The two of them had made no effort to keep things between them a secret from their coworkers the last couple of weeks.

"I like to think Dylan and I are really good friends," Katie answered.

"Friends, huh? That's not what Violet is

telling everyone," Summer said. "She seems to think she's going to be getting a new mother soon."

Katie was stunned into silence. The only person that Dylan hadn't wanted to know they were involved, at least more than friends, was Violet. "I don't know why she would say something like that. We've been very careful not to give her any reason to believe that we're anything more than friends."

"She's an eight-year-old girl who watches princess movies. She sees romance as big fancy weddings where the prince and princess live happily ever after," Jo said with a bitterness that left no doubt there was a story there.

"But she's also an eight-year-old girl whose mother just dropped her off one day with a father who was a stranger. Not that it was Dylan's fault. He had no idea that he had a kid out there," Summer said. "That wasn't fair to either one of them."

"Dylan worships that little girl. Neither one of us want to hurt her." She'd have to let Dylan know what Violet was saying so she could have a talk with his daughter and explain their friendship. Violet was the most important person in Dylan's life, as it should be. He didn't want his little girl confused by another person leaving her, especially if she'd had hopes that Katie would be staying forever. This wasn't good.

"So now that we know the two of you don't have plans to rush down the aisle of matrimony, what exactly is going on? I've seen the looks you two exchange when you don't think anyone's watching you. And by the way, you should know that everybody is watching you," Jo added. "Just like everybody is watching Summer and Alex."

"Alex? I don't see any Alex, do you?" Summer snapped before slouching down in her seat. "I've had one phone call and half a dozen texts in the last six weeks and none of them have explained where he is and when he's coming back. What could be so secretive that he can't answer a simple question about where he is? It's not like he's on some secret military mission. I know. I asked him."

"You asked him about a secret military mission? Did you really think he'd tell you the truth if he was? It's called a secret mission for a reason," Jo pointed out, laughing at her friend as they slowed down to drive through one of the many small keys between Key West and Miami.

"Have you asked Dylan? I think he's received a couple emails," Katie said.

"I have. He says he doesn't know any more than I do." Summer shrugged. "So back to you and Dylan, do you think you'll see each other when you return to New York?"

"We haven't discussed it." She didn't think that maintaining a relationship with that many miles between them would appeal to Dylan. What would they do, take turns flying out to see each other every month or two? She couldn't begin to imagine her beach-loving lover in the middle of New York surrounded by skyscrapers. Besides, there was Violet. She'd be more confused than she was now. They couldn't do that to the child.

"I can understand that. It's hard to maintain a long-distance relationship," Jo said.

"Especially, when you don't even know where the person you are supposed to be in a relationship with might be," Summer put in.

"How come nobody told me about you and Alex?" Katie asked. It seemed odd that everyone knew the two of them were involved but never mentioned it to her.

"Well, first, we weren't sure what your past relationship with Alex had been. Second, nobody but me, and now you, know that there is definitely something going on between the two of them," Jo said.

"The only thing between me and Alex is friendship. We worked together when he lived in New York. For full disclosure, I'll admit we did attend a Heli-Care corporate function together once, but that was all. I like Alex, but he kind of reminds me of my brothers," Katie said.

"Maybe you should introduce me to one of your brothers," Summer deadpanned.

"Hold on a minute. You have a man," Jo said.

"I don't see one. Do you?" Summer turned around to face Katie in the back seat.

"I have four brothers, but only two of them are single," Katie said.

They spent the rest of the trip with Katie telling them stories of growing up in a house full of men, and Jo teasing Summer about which brother would be the better catch. Jo insisted that Summer would be better off with a lawyer than a policeman. It was plain to see that Jo was trying to cheer up her friend.

By the time they hit the stores, they were all feeling the need to let off some steam, which apparently meant buying as much merchandise as could be squeezed into Jo's compact car.

They made the trip home surrounded by shoeboxes and bags of clothes and accessories. When Katie questioned their shopping habits, she was quickly informed that they only bought items on sale and they only went on a buying spree once every three months. It still seemed like more clothes than the two women could wear in a year, but what did she know? She hadn't had a mother to teach her how to shop. Her father had been a believer of having two pairs of shoes, and an outfit for each day of the week. She'd spent all her money on paints and canvases instead of fancy dresses and makeup.

The thought of her growing up without a mother reminded her of Violet. Either she or Dylan would have to speak with her. Her friend's explanations that Violet was just a little girl that read romance everywhere made sense. Katie and Dylan had spent a lot of time together the last few weeks. It could be that the child was just confused by what she saw between the two adults. Katie didn't want to think of Violet being hurt by something she misread that Katie had done.

It was late when she made her way to her front door carrying the few packages that she had bought. The lights at Dylan's place were out. She'd have to wait until the next day to speak with him about his daughter. She only hoped that he'd be able to explain his and Katie's relationship to Violet better than she'd been able to explain it to Jo and Summer. But then, maybe the problem was she didn't really have words for what was between the two of them herself.

Katie didn't know what she'd expected on Gallery Night, but this hadn't been it. Strings of tiny fairy lights ran the length of the art gallery shops staying open late for the night while other artists had set up stalls on the sidewalk, giving it a magical atmosphere with a French flair.

When Jo had talked her into buying the rose-colored maxi dress with its thin spaghetti straps for her night with Dylan, she'd thought her new friend was mistaken. She'd been to Duval Street just a few days ago where the average attire had been shorts and comfortable T's. Now as they joined the women dressed in cocktail dresses and men in dressed slacks and ties, she was glad she had listened. The attire would have fit into any New York five-star restaurant. The atmosphere was much more welcoming than any party she'd ever attended.

Just the walk from the parking lot had made her thankful that she had not listened to Jo when she tried to insist that Katie buy a pair of four-inch heels to go with the dress. Katie had gone with the two inch. It had been the smart choice.

She had slept in and missed seeing Dylan until he arrived at her door that night. She knew she had to broach the subject of Violet and her misunderstanding about their future, but she didn't want the magic of the night to be interrupted. Violet was staying with her grandparents for the night. There would be no reason for Dylan to sleep at his house alone. As they walked the sidewalks admiring each artist's wares, a sexual anticipation was building between them…

Dylan's hand skimmed across her waist and she shuddered.

"You okay?" he asked. His eyes looked down at her with a protectiveness that touched her heart. "If the crowds are too much, we can go."

"It was just the breeze," Katie said. How did she tell the man that the mere touch of his hand was setting her body on fire?

She'd never felt anything like the need she felt for Dylan, both in and out of the bedroom. Would this ever fade? She was afraid that it wouldn't. And what would that mean for her? Would she be walking around New York like a zombie? Dead to all of life except for her job? Her only hope was that distance would make her see things more clearly.

A group of teenage tourists rushed past them and they were pushed into a small alley. Dylan's hands came around her waist and she leaned back into him as he wrapped his arms around her. Her head fell back against his shoulder and she breathed in the scent of him. Would she ever smell the breeze off the ocean and not think of him?

"We can leave whenever you're ready," Dylan murmured. The gold flecks in his green eyes reflected the light from the low-hanging string of lights over their heads. Wearing dress slacks and shirt, he could have adorned the advertisement billboards of Time Square.

And he only had eyes for her. She felt like one of Violet's princesses out for the night with her prince. Thank goodness the little girl wasn't there, because at that moment Katie knew anyone who saw them would think the two of them were in love. It was a good thing they had agreed to no complications in their relationship. Otherwise, she too might have thought Dylan had love in his eyes at that moment.

But they'd taken love off the table. Dylan had broken one rule by getting involved with her in the first place. She was sure he wouldn't break another one. They'd been up-front with their expectations in their relationship. When she returned to New York their relationship would be over no matter how much daydreaming she'd been doing.

"Katie?" he asked as he laid his forehead to hers. "Are you okay? We've seen most of the artists. We've can leave if you're ready."

No. She wasn't okay. She'd probably never

be okay once she left this island and Dylan. She should pull back from him, start getting used to the distance that would soon separate the two of them, but she wasn't that strong. She wanted the time they had left together. She wanted this one night alone. She wanted it to never end.

"I'm fine," she said. Her lips brushed his. His teeth grazed her bottom lip as he gave it a little nip and pulled her tighter against him. His hard length pressed against her. Desire shot through her.

"We're almost to the end of the block, but I'm ready if you are." Her body was aching to take him in right there.

"We can see the rest of the artists another time," he said as he took her hand, all but hauling her out onto the street.

Did he even understand what he said? Didn't he realize that there wouldn't be another chance for her to see the other artists? She'd be back in New York before the next Gallery Night.

CHAPTER ELEVEN

KATIE DIDN'T KNOW why she felt so nervous. She and Dylan had made love several times. It wasn't their first night together. But it could probably be the last time Dylan got to spend the night with her. She'd come to love those few mornings that she'd woken up to find Dylan asleep next to her. They even had a routine where she got up early to do her yoga and meditation, something that helped her tune into her mental health needs, and he'd later join her with her first cup of coffee for the day. They'd sit back on the porch and watch the trees come alive as the birds started their own day traveling from tree to tree.

She had begun to think of it as their time. That early morning time when it was just the two of them before they had to deal with disruptive phone calls and the other daily chores of living. She could see how dangerous that had been now. She'd been thinking of them as a couple. She'd let herself get caught up in emotions that she had no right having.

But the idea of distancing themselves as they transitioned into being separated held no appeal right then. What did it matter? The damage was done. Her memories of their time alone would be all she was taking when she left Key West.

She stepped out of the bathroom wearing a silky gown of white. It covered the top of her thighs and had thin straps and a dipped neck. It covered all of the important parts, but it clung to them too.

"I feel stupid," she said as she stood against the bathroom door while Dylan lay on his side of the bed staring at her. "It's Jo's fault. She's the one that talked me into buying it."

"I'll have to see about getting the woman a raise," Dylan said. "I loved the gown you were wearing tonight, but this? You look amazing."

"It's not something that I would normally wear. The gown I wore tonight, I mean. I'm not somebody that dresses up all the time."

She walked over to the bed and sat down next to him.

"No, you're one of New York City's heroes who is more at home in a blue flight suit saving lives than dressing up for a dinner party," he said as he pulled her down to lay beside her.

How could someone who had only known her for a few weeks understand who she was better than some of the friends she had known a lifetime?

He'd taken off his dress shirt and removed his belt. Turning into his arms, she felt what could only be described as grief for what they could have had together if it weren't for the two of them being from different worlds.

His fingers tipped her chin up to meet his eyes. "I feel like you're already leaving me."

"I feel like I'm watching an hourglass as the sand streams down faster and faster." She didn't want to ruin the night, but she had to share how she felt with him.

"We have the whole night. Give us this night. We have enough sand to last a lifetime right outside your door. Let's not worry about the ones that are falling tonight." Dylan brushed her hair back from her face.

What did he mean by enough sand for a lifetime? Was he saying that they could have more time together?

"Let's make some memories together tonight," he murmured.

He peeled down one strap of her gown and the other, exposing her breast to the cool breeze that flowed into the room from an open window. Her mouth was suddenly dry and she couldn't speak.

His hand cupped her left breast and stayed there for a moment. Her heart rate doubled then skipped a beat under his palm when his other hand began to move up her thighs.

She drew in a deep breath. Her body pressed up against his, waiting for the touch of his fingers on her most intimate parts. The touch that would drive her to madness.

His smile was one of satisfaction. He knew that she wanted him. But Katie had never been a passive woman. Not with her brothers, not with her job, and certainly not in the bedroom.

"Lose the pants," she ordered, then watched as he stripped for her.

Her fingers were around him before he could take his place beside her. He pulsed against her hand. She wasn't the only one who suffered from the madness that drove them into a feverish lovemaking.

She'd thought they would make slow and sweet love tonight, but the need to have him inside her had taken away all her control. They had the rest of the night. She wanted him now.

His mouth was on her breast then, her nipples both hard and throbbing. His hand tortured her as it slid in then out of her wet folds.

She was so close to coming, but she needed more. She wanted to make their memory a spectacular one. One that would make sure he never forgot her.

When he started to cover her, she surprised him. Pushing him onto his back instead of pulling him down to her.

"My turn," she said as she straddled him.

"I'm all yours," he said, relaxing under her with a smile that took her breath away. Lying there, stretched out before her with those sexy curls falling around his face, her heart swelled with an emotion she wouldn't name. There was no future in it. No future at all for them. They had this moment. It was all she was assured and she wasn't going to waste it.

She bent over him, her hair a curtain that brushed against his chest before she placed a soft kiss against his lips. Three little words swirled through her mind, but she wouldn't let herself utter them.

His arms came around her, pulling her down against him as the kiss became more demanding, as seconds became minutes, as the kiss went from searching to passionate only ending when they were both too breathless to continue.

Pushing up with arms and legs that trembled with desire she stared down at him. This man brought out a passionate side of her that she hadn't known existed.

She lowered herself onto him, inch by inch, his arms gripping her waist, and his gaze hot and fierce as he filled her. Removing his hands from her waist, she locked her fingers with his. She would let him see the woman that she was, strong and not afraid to take charge.

Rocking against him, she lost herself in the rhythm as he matched her every movement. His strong body arching up to meet her soft one, as they became one if only for this short time.

She'd lost her grip on his hands, but she wasn't sure how. All she knew was the feel of Dylan's fingers as he stroked between her legs.

Pleasure swelled inside her, intensifying until her breath caught in a climax that caught them both in its grip as they came together in a sensual satisfaction that she had never experienced before.

She collapsed on top of Dylan, her body boneless, her muscles failing to keep her upright. As Dylan held her, she wept.

When the phone rang the next morning, Katie did not answer it on the first ring or the second ring. Buried beneath a combination of covers and limbs, she didn't want to move. She wasn't on duty today.

She stretched her legs as best she could with one heavily muscled thigh thrown across her. She couldn't even work if she was needed. She and Dylan had spent most of the night in each other's arms. Their lovemaking had gone from fierce to soft and then back to demanding. When Dylan said he wanted to make memories of the night, he wasn't joking. The world outside her window started to lighten with the soft gray tones of dawn when they'd finally fallen asleep.

Her phone rang again.

Moaning, she lifted Dylan's arm and scooted out from under his thigh before grabbing her gown from the floor and picking up her phone. The number was from New York. Couldn't she have one night of sex without being bothered by one of her brothers?

She shut the bedroom door behind her before she answered.

"Good morning, Matt. I'm surprised to hear from you this time of morning. You just getting off shift?" she asked. Her night shift–loving brother was known to be grumpy in the early morning hours.

"Katie, it's…it's Junior," Matt said, his tone steady as only a man used to relaying bad news could be. She knew that tone. She lived in a world where conveying bad news was part of the job.

"Matt, what's wrong? What's happened to Junior?" Her voice quivered but she refused to break down. Not until she knew how bad things were.

"Another warrant went out for the guy that shot you. We've been putting the pressure on him and we got a tip he was involved in a drug deal that went down last night. We pulled the tape of the area and caught him making the exchange. Junior and I wanted to be there when they arrested him." The longer her brother talked the more his voice broke. There wasn't much that would make her street-tough brother break down.

"Is he alive?" Katie asked, unable to listen to any more information. She just needed to know that her brother was alive.

"He's in surgery. He took a shot to the gut. In and out the doctor said, but it did a lot of damage going through. He said they lost him once in the emergency room. Blood loss. They were doing some rapid transfusion thing on him. Said it saved his life."

He would be okay. Her brother was in surgery now and they'd do whatever repairs that were needed. They had to. She couldn't lose her brother. Not like this.

"You need to come, Katie. You need to come home. Dad's not looking so good. We need you here."

"I'll catch the next flight. Tell Daddy, I'll

be home as soon as I can. I'll call you when I get to the airport." Katie hit the button to hang up. Then looked around the room. She didn't know what to do first.

"What's happened?" Dylan asked from the bedroom door. "Katie?"

Her mind tried to wrap around everything Matt had just told her, but none of it was making sense.

"Junior went to arrest the guy who they arrested earlier for shooting me, and the guy shot my brother." She wanted to blame the judge who'd let a dangerous killer out on bail. She wanted to take the blame herself for being the reason her brother had been shot. But none of that would help John Jr. right then. She needed to concentrate on getting to New York as fast as possible.

"I've got to get home," she said as she grabbed her laptop off the kitchen island. She punched in her password. "I need a flight from here that I can take?"

"I think there's one flight a day that's directly to New York. Go pack and I'll see what I can find out." Dylan already had his phone out.

"Okay, thanks," she said and rushed back into the bedroom.

She didn't know where to start. She'd brought so much stuff with her. Her clothes, books, her paints. She had no idea how long she would be gone.

But she didn't have to take everything now. She'd have to come back for the Jeep anyway. She could get everything she had to have in one bag and a carry-on.

She pulled her suitcase out of the closet and opened it on the bed. If she missed the one flight out to New York, she'd have Dylan drive her to Miami where there would be more available flights.

She dumped a drawer of underwear into the suitcase then followed it with one full of shirts and shorts.

"Your ticket is waiting at the airport," Dylan said as he bent to pick up a T-shirt she'd dropped.

"How long do I have?" she asked as she shut her suitcase then pulled out her carry-on bag.

He followed her into the kitchen where she grabbed her computer and vitamins. "You have an hour till boarding."

"I'll never make it." She looked down and saw that she still wore her nightgown.

"Go change and I'll load the bags. You forget that we're just a little island. I can have you there in fifteen minutes, ten if traffic isn't heavy."

"But I have to get my bags checked and go through security." She pulled a pair of jeans and a T-shirt out of the closet and rushed into the bathroom.

She stuck her brush and makeup into her carry-on. She could deal with that on the way. She picked the gown she'd worn the night before off the counter where she had laid it. She didn't have any need for it in New York, but she couldn't bring herself to leave it behind. Who knew what would happen in New York? She could be there for weeks.

She slid her feet into sandals and hefted her carry-on onto her shoulder. She wanted to take a last look at the cottage. She wanted to walk onto her deck and breathe in the air one more time. But time wasn't something she had right now.

When she stepped out into the sunshine to join Dylan, the rush of adrenaline that she'd been burning gave out. Was this goodbye?

She locked the door to her little cottage with a finality that she wasn't prepared for. She had no idea how long she'd be needed in New York.

The ride to the airport was fast and it wasn't until they stood on the sidewalk outside that she realized Dylan had come to the same conclusion: this could be the goodbye they had known was coming. It wasn't fair that it was coming now, though. She wasn't ready to say goodbye yet.

They'd made plans for a trip to the beach after Violet came home from her sleepover. Violet. She had planned to tell Dylan about Violet's statements to Jo this morning.

"Oh, Dylan. I need to tell you something. I shouldn't have waited, but…it was just… and now I'm leaving…"

"Katie, there's no time. Your plane will be boarding in a few minutes. You need to go."

"But it's Violet. I was going to talk to you this morning about what Jo told me, but we didn't have the time." She knew she was just making excuses for not speaking about it earlier, when the truth was she'd been afraid that Dylan would want to end things between them after she told him. "But you need to know this, especially now."

"What about Violet?" he asked, his eyes, which had been avoiding her since they left the cottage, now locked with hers.

"Jo says she's gotten it into her mind that you and I, that the two of us, are a couple. She seems to think that I'm going to stay and that we're going to get married."

"And now I have to tell her you're leaving?" The shock on his face quickly turned to pain. She knew it had been his greatest fear that his daughter would be hurt.

He turned away to take her suitcase from the back seat of his car. It wasn't until they were at the airport doors that he spoke.

"I'll take care of getting the rest of your belongings packed and shipped," Dylan said as he handed the handle to her.

"I'm still on the schedule," she said. "And there's the Jeep."

"I'll take care of it. You don't need to worry about things here. Take care of your family," he said then pointed to the ticker board inside the entrance. "You better hurry or you'll miss your flight."

But still she stood there. Was this really

how it ended? Was he not even going to kiss her goodbye?

He was angry. At her? At himself for not protecting his daughter? Did it really matter when she didn't even know if she would ever see him again.

She grabbed him by the shirt and pulled him to her. He might be ready to let things end between them as strangers, but she wasn't. He meant too much to her.

She pressed her lips to his and gave him a deep kiss that he was not going to forget easily before turning and running to make her plane.

CHAPTER TWELVE

It didn't take Katie but a moment to find her father and brothers in the surgical ICU waiting room that was crowded with NYPD officers, both uniformed and plainclothes.

"Katie, you're here," her youngest brother shouted, making his way to her. A sob escaped her lips as he caught her up in his arms.

"How is he?" she asked. Her brother had still been in surgery when she'd touched down in New York.

"He just got out of surgery. The bullet did a lot of damage, but the doctor says he stopped all the bleeding," Mikey said, as he led her over to the corner where her father stood waiting.

"Oh, Daddy," she choked, as she was once again wrapped inside strong arms.

"He's going to be okay," her father said, though she didn't know if he was talking to himself or her.

"Lisa just went back to see him," Mikey said as Katie took a seat beside him.

"How is she holding up?" Katie asked. His brother's fiancée, a district attorney, was as tough as they came.

Before anyone could answer, Katie saw the petite blonde woman they'd been discussing enter the waiting room and head toward them.

"He's going to be okay. He's sleeping and they said they were going to leave him on the ventilator until tomorrow, but they say he's stable," Lisa said, breathless as she rushed toward them then suddenly broke into tears.

Katie gathered her into her arms while the other McGee men walked off using the excuse that they needed to tell the other officers the good news.

"They're all alike," Lisa laughed as she wiped her tears away. "They're ready to run into a burning building or fight their way through a hail of bullets to rescue someone, but as soon as a woman sheds a few tears they run the other way."

"I know," Katie said as the two of them moved apart.

"Thanks for understanding. It was just seeing him lying there. He was so still. You know Junior. He's never still. It just scared me." Lisa wiped at her eyes, then looked up at Katie. "They explained all the monitors to me and they say he's stable, but I told his nurse you were a flight nurse with Heli-Care. He promised to let you come in whenever you arrived. I thought maybe you could go check him out. You know. Just to be sure he's doing okay."

"Oh, okay." Katie stood, anxious to see her brother and reassure all of them that he truly was going to be okay.

It wasn't until a few minutes later, standing over her brother, that it hit her: only months ago she had lain in a similar room recovering from a gunshot wound much too similar to her brother's. The sight of her strong older brother pale and unmoving against the white hospital linen made her feel sick.

She waited for the anxiety that she dreaded to hit her, but it didn't come. If this had happened six weeks ago, she knew that she would not have been able to stand there. All the work she had done with her counselor and the confidence she'd rebuilt with Dylan's help made the difference.

After checking her brother's ventilator settings and reviewing his vital signs with his brother's nurse until she was satisfied that Junior was recovering as he should be, she made her way back to where her family waited for her.

Dylan sat on the steps to Katie's cottage and waited for his daughter's bus to arrive. No, not Katie's cottage. Katie was gone. And it had never really been Katie's cottage. She'd always been just a temporary renter. Just like, they had been temporary lovers.

Only it hadn't ever felt temporary. What they had together had grown when it shouldn't have. That was his mistake. Instead of keeping things light and friendly between the two of them, he'd crossed the line to caring about Katie as more than just a lover. Something that hadn't been in their agreement. There was a reason he had rules for his love life which included not getting involved with someone who was visiting the island. But he'd broken the rule and now he had to live with the consequences.

He had always known Katie's plan was to return to New York. Not only was her family and life there, he knew a part of Katie wanted to prove to herself that she'd made it back to being one of the best flight nurses in the biggest city in the country. Her confidence had been so low when she'd first arrived. He wasn't sure even Katie had believed she would recover enough to become the nurse she had been before. But something about the stubborn tilt of that chin of hers had told him that she wasn't a woman who was going to give up. Her determination was one of the things he loved about her.

He stood and swore. Love wasn't part of their agreement. Thank goodness he'd never let on to Katie about the way he felt. She had made it plain that she didn't want any complications any more than he did. Her goal was to get back to New York. His was to protect his daughter.

From what Katie had told him, he had failed.

The yellow bus came to a stop at the top of the drive. The pride he felt when his daughter ran up to him and hugged him eased some of the pain in his chest. He was so lucky to have Violet. Her mother could have kept her away from him forever. But Lilly had done the right thing for her daughter, bringing her to him. The little girl needed a stable home.

"Hey, Daddy, can we go inside and see Katie? I brought another book home from the library that I think she'll like." Violet stared up at him with the light blue eyes of her mother.

"She's not here, honey," he said.

"Did she go off with Jo and Summer shopping again?" Violet followed him as they made the walk from Katie's cottage. "Can I go next time? Jo promised to help me pick some new clothes."

"We'll see about you going with Jo, but Katie won't be able to go. A bad man hurt her brother and she had to go home." Dylan opened the door to the house and watched as his daughter hung her backpack in the small closet at their entrance without being told. She was taking Katie's leaving a lot better than he thought she would. Maybe Jo was mistaken about what Violet had said.

"That's okay. I can wait till she gets back,"

his daughter said as she shut the door. "My jeans are just a little short. It'll be okay."

"No, Violet, I don't think you understand. Katie isn't coming back. She would have told you goodbye but her brother is hurt really bad. She had to take the first flight she could get to take her home to New York." Dylan saw the moment his daughter understood his words. Once more he was left alone to pick up the pieces, only this time it wouldn't be just his heart, it would also be his daughter's.

Then she smiled and laughed. "Katie can't have left for good. She left her car. Besides, she can't stay in New York when you get married. She has to come back and live with us."

"Baby, what makes you think that Katie and I are getting married?" He'd searched his mind for some action or something he could have said that might have caused his daughter to come to this conclusion, but there wasn't anything.

"Nobody told me. But I saw you kissing her when you thought I was asleep. You were out on the deck. Don't you remember?" Violet asked.

He did remember being out on the deck

one night when Violet had gotten up for a drink. Had his daughter been spying on him? But that still didn't explain why she thought they were getting married. She was much too young to understand his and Katie's friendship.

"Violet, come sit next to me on the couch." How was he supposed to do this? Was there a handbook out there for single dads with a chapter on how to keep your child from dreaming up romantic ideas concerning your love life? He took a deep breath.

"Honey, sometimes men and women kiss each other when they're just friends. It doesn't mean that they are going to get married. It can just be a way to show that you like someone." There. Simple and to the point. If only things between him and Katie could be that simple.

"I like Shawn Hart at school, sometimes. Does that mean I have to kiss him?" his daughter asked.

"No. Definitely not. There is not to be any kissing Shawn Hart or anybody else." He was messing this all up. He needed to take control of this talk before it ended up in places he was not ready to go.

"Look. The bottom line is that Katie and I aren't getting married. She has a life in New York that she had to get back to. My life is here with you. We'll both miss her, but we'll be okay."

"Don't worry, Daddy, Katie will be back soon. You'll see," Violet said before giving him a look which he knew meant her mind was made up and there was nothing he could say that was going to change it.

Katie scrolled through her texts, stopping at the only text she had received from Dylan since she'd left Key West and rereading it as she had every few hours for the last two days.

How is your brother?

He's doing better than expected. He's being extubated this morning and should move out of the critical care unit this morning. How is Violet?

OK

She'd waited for him to expand on his answer, but nothing else came. Those two little letters seemed to have been all he had to say to her. And now she didn't know what to do.

She'd typed message after message back to him, then deleted each one before she sent them. His last words of assurance that she didn't need to worry about things in Key West, had seemed final.

Her door buzzed and she looked out to see that it was her father.

"What's happened?" she asked as she flung the door open. She'd just talked to her brother and he seemed to be doing well.

"Everything's fine. I just wanted a few minutes alone with my daughter away from that crowded waiting room," her father said as he walked past her into her apartment. "Could I get a cup of coffee?"

There were dark circles under her father's eyes and his usually perfectly pressed uniform looked as if he'd been wearing it for days. She remembered him looking like this only once before. Then, it had been her in the hospital that he'd been worrying over. "I think you need a nap instead of more coffee."

"Coffee for now, if you don't mind. I can sleep later," he said, though he did take a seat in the nearest chair.

After starting the coffee, she returned to her father. "Really, Daddy, it's okay for you to take a break. Junior's doing fine now."

"I know. I'm headed home after I leave here. I just had to make a trip to the courthouse to make sure no judge was going to let that shooter out again. The man shot two of my kids. *Two.*" Her father stood with those words and headed into her kitchen. She knew the coffee was only an excuse for him to leave the room. He'd been raised in a time when men didn't let others see any sign of weakness. She allowed him a few minutes of privacy before she joined him.

"So when are you headed back to Key West?" her father asked.

Startled, her first sip of coffee went down wrong causing a fit of coughing that took several seconds to recover from.

"I don't think I am," she said, setting her cup down and wiping the countertop for the umpteenth time that morning.

"Didn't your contract go until the first of the month? Shouldn't you be returning to finish it?" her father asked.

"Are you in a hurry to get rid of me?" she asked. Her father seldom made small talk.

There was a reason he made the trip to see her but there would be no hurrying him to get to it.

"Of course not. I like having all my kids where I can get to them if they need me."

It was a very fatherly thing for him to say and she knew it was true. Dylan had expressed the same sentiment when he'd worried about not having the legal paperwork giving him full custody of Violet. Lilly could take their daughter at any time and he wouldn't be able to guarantee her safety.

"If you don't want to finish your contract, that's up to you. You've got to return anyway, don't you? That Jeep isn't going to drive itself back to New York."

Her father was right. While Dylan had offered to pack her things, a plane ticket to Key West would be much cheaper.

But returning to Key West would mean more goodbyes.

"Besides, your brothers say you seemed happy there. More like the old Katie," her father said.

"You mean more like the way I was before I was shot?" she asked. Her father was as uncomfortable discussing that night as she had been. But that was before she'd gone to Key West. Before the work she'd done with her counselor. Before she'd had Dylan on her side encouraging her to do the work that was needed for her recovery.

"It's okay to say it. I won't break if we talk about it." Not now. Never again. No matter how hard it was to acknowledge, she would never hide from that night again. She'd given it power over her by keeping what happened that night in the dark. But now that she had brought it all out into the light, she knew that, though she would never be the same, she could be just as strong if not stronger.

"I should have talked to you sooner. It was just such a shock. With your brothers, I've always known there was a chance of them being injured. But you? This wasn't supposed to happen to you."

She stepped toward her father and wrapped her arms around him. "It's okay, Daddy. I'm going to be okay. So is Junior."

Then for the first time since the shooting, she and her dad sat at her little kitchen table and talked openly about what happened the night she'd been hurt and the way it had affected her.

An hour later, after her father had promised that he would go straight home to rest and she had assured him that she would never let her fear of worrying him keep her from confiding in him, they said their tearful goodbyes and she returned to her phone where she saw she had received a new text from Jo.

Dylan told us what happened to you brother. How is he? Are you okay?

Katie didn't think twice before she returned the text. Her father was right.

He's doing great. See you soon.

Putting away her phone, she headed to her bedroom to pack.

CHAPTER THIRTEEN

"KATIE!" VIOLET CRIED as she sprang out of the car and ran up the steps of the rental cottage.

Dylan had known Katie was returning to the island—Jo had spread the word to all the crew—but he still wasn't prepared to see her. He'd spent hours staring out his window at the cottage, knowing she would never return. But she had.

For just a moment, seeing her standing there, her hair blowing in the soft gulf breeze, her lips curved into a big smile for the two of them, he felt a momentary jolt of hope. And then he saw her suitcase and was reminded she'd only returned to finish out her contract. She'd be leaving again.

And he'd have to go through the same hell as he had when he'd watched her turn from him at the airport. His hand instinctively brushed against his lips as he remembered the kiss she'd given him before she'd run away. It wasn't one he would ever be able to forget.

Which was just more reason for him to stay away from her now. Memories that he'd thought would give him some relief from the pain of her leaving, now haunted him instead.

"Hello," Katie said, as she started down the stairs toward him.

"Your brother must be doing okay," he said as he made it to his daughter and put his arm around her shoulders.

"They're releasing him from the hospital tomorrow." She looked almost as uncomfortable as he felt.

"See, Daddy. I told you Katie was coming back," Violet said matter-of-factly.

"I see. Didn't you say you needed to start on your geography homework as soon as you got home?" He didn't need his daughter bringing up all her wildly romantic notions in front of Katie. Things were awkward enough between the two of them.

"I know. I just wanted to talk to Katie for

a minute. Maybe she can come over for supper?" his daughter asked, her eyes pleading with him.

"We're eating at your grandparents' house tonight," he said quickly, knowing he'd have to make a quick call to his mother to warn her of their new plans.

He couldn't do anything that might encourage Violet's idea that he and Katie were a couple. Instead, he needed to remind his daughter that Katie was just here temporarily and the two of them were only friends.

"It sounds like you have a very busy evening ahead of you," Katie said to Violet before turning toward him. "I checked the schedule and saw I'm on for the four shifts next week."

"Jo and Casey took some time off and I figured you wouldn't mind since it's your last week," Dylan said, aware Violet was listening intently to every word. It was time his daughter accepted that Katie would not be staying.

"It's not a problem," Katie said before addressing Violet. "How about we get together next week for a painting day? If it's okay with your daddy, of course."

Dylan met Katie's eyes and knew he couldn't deny either one of them that one last day together.

"That would be fine. But right now, we both better go get ready before it's time for us to leave for my parents' home." He turned Violet toward their own home, making his escape as painless as possible.

As they reached the top of the steps, Violet turned to wave goodbye to Katie. Unable to help himself, he turned too, catching sight of Katie disappearing into the cottage.

It was Katie's last flight in Key West. In a couple more hours she would be clocking out for the last time. For now, though, she had no choice than to sit next to a somber Dylan, who had done a great job of pretending she didn't exist for the last week. As soon as the helicopter skids lifted off the ground, her stomach had begun to churn and it wasn't because of the speed at which they flew across the island.

"Hang on, guys," Roy said over their headphones. "This is going to be a quick trip."

As Dylan was lead, Katie prepared their

scene bag, checking to make sure everything was in place.

"Miami General is accepting," Dylan said over the headphones. "They're notifying their neurosurgeon now."

"This place has a reputation for being rough so the county cops are securing the scene right now. They've got the suspect in custody, but it seems there was a drunken brawl in progress when they arrived," Roy said as he banked to the left.

The local fire department for the small lower key came over the radio with the coordinates of their landing zone and Roy had them landing only six minutes from takeoff.

"Where's our patient?" Dylan asked one of the officers who'd been designated to escort them. It seemed that though the fighting had stopped, the amount of inebriated customers had them all on alert.

"This way," the young officer said, leading them up to a large shack made up of large poles and what looked like palm limbs.

"They called this a bar?" Katie asked Dylan as they walked through the sand along the path through all the onlookers.

"It's a tiki bar. They're popular with the tourists," Dylan explained, speaking directly to her for the first time in days.

Following the officer, she was surprised to see that their patient now lay on top of the bar while an older woman, the only person besides the first responders who seemed to be sober, was wiping up blood with her bar towel. The scene was wrong in so many ways.

"Let's get this guy and get out of here," she told Dylan.

"It's okay. They're just drunk. The officers can handle them," Dylan said as he put a hand on her waist and gently urged her in front of him.

Startled by his touch, she jumped. Even through her thick flight suit, the one that had been made to strict specifications to protect her from the hottest of fires, couldn't protect her from the feel of his hand against her.

But as they took the last few steps up to the bar, she realized why Dylan had suddenly become so attentive. He thought she was reacting to the crowd that surrounded her. She wanted to laugh, but it hurt too much. Only when he thought she needed him to help her through her anxiety had he been ready to give her the attention she craved since she arrived back in the keys.

"It's not them," she said as she pulled away from him and pointed back to the crowd that was beginning to thin as the officers explained the bar was closed for the night. Or early morning as was the case.

"It's her," Katie said, pointing to the woman, who was now straightening the back of the bar, ignoring the unconscious man stretched across her bar being cared for by the local ambulance crew. "That's cold. Scary cold."

Dylan looked at the woman and nodded his head before moving in front of Katie and beginning his assessment of their patient. Maybe it would have been better if she had pretended the crowd was the trouble. At least then she wouldn't have to deal with the cold shoulder Dylan had been giving her.

Though she expected the patient's injuries were superficial except for what looked like an orbital fracture, she started an intravenous line in each arm and prepared to infuse a bag of fluid.

"Let's get him loaded," Dylan said after he finished bandaging a nasty-looking cut across the man's hand.

It wasn't until they were back on their way from Miami while she was staring out the window that it truly hit her: this would be the last time she flew across the beautiful body of water below her.

It was also the last time she'd sit next to Dylan, crammed into the two seats next to each other, something that she'd always enjoyed. Until now. The feel of his hand against her waist had brought back the deep need and desire that had once consumed her. Had it affected him the same way it had her? There was a time when she would have felt comfortable asking him, exploring those needs and desires. But that was before he froze her out.

It was a good thing that tomorrow would be her last day on the island before she packed up and left for New York, because she didn't think she could take any more of Dylan ignoring what they'd had such a short time ago. Had it just been a a couple months ago, that she'd been driven to seek some distance from her home in order to heal? And now she was running the opposite way.

Sometimes life just didn't make sense.

CHAPTER FOURTEEN

DYLAN HAD LISTENED to the laughter coming from Katie's back deck all morning. Most of it had been his daughter's giggles, but occasionally he heard the sweet sound of Katie's own laughter above his daughter's.

He could have shut the door to his back deck, closed the windows he had opened to let the fresh air in, or gone into one of the other rooms where he couldn't hear the two of them. Instead, he'd chosen to let the music of their voices fill his home as he went through his weekend chores. It was a masochistic thing to do. He knew that. But he wasn't strong enough to pretend that he didn't enjoy the sound of the two of them as they painted and talked.

He knew it was only his threats of taking away her allotted television time that kept his daughter from making any comments about Kate's leaving. Trying to explain to his eight-year-old that real adult relationships didn't work like the animated movies she loved hadn't gone well.

The knock on the back door jarred him back into the present as his daughter raced by him to her room carrying several large pieces of paper.

"Hi," Katie said as she stepped into the house. She carried a canvas but had it turned away from him. "I'm sorry. I was trying to explain to her that I had finished my contract and had to go home."

His daughter's door slammed behind her and the two of them were left alone. He'd known this was coming. At least he'dd prepared as much as any father could prepare for their daughter's heart to be broken.

"I know. I don't blame you." He blamed himself. He'd known no matter what, Katie leaving both of their lives would be hard. It was like Lilly leaving Violet all over again.

"I wanted to give you this. I know you said you liked it, though if you don't want to hang it I'll understand."

He took the canvas she held out to him

and was surprised to see it was the painting of the white heron that she'd been so excited about. "Are you sure you don't want to take it with you?"

"I've got another one I'm taking with me. I've also got some supplies for Violet that I'm going to leave in the cottage." She looked down at her feet then back up to him. "I want to thank you for everything you've done. I mean..."

Her face flushed pink. "I mean I needed a friend when I got here. Thanks for being there. For being that friend."

What was he to say to that? How could she compare what they'd had to merely friendship?

"I've got to go. I'm meeting Jo and Summer downtown in a few hours."

Holding the canvas, he stood and watched as she rushed away. Had those been tears in her eyes?

"Why didn't you ask her to stay?" Violet demanded from behind him. "She loves me and you. I know she does. Ask her. She'll tell you."

He should have known his daughter would

be listening to their conversation. "That's not the kind of thing you ask someone, honey."

"How doyou know if she would have stayed when you didn't ask her?" His daughter's voice was getting louder.

Why was she angry at him? He wasn't the one leaving.

"You didn't ask Katie to stay just like you didn't ask my mommy to stay." His daughter cried.

"Oh, baby," he said as he bent down and took his daughter into his arms. "Your mommy couldn't stay. She would be miserable here. We both knew it. But it wasn't because she didn't love you. She just can't be happy in one place for very long."

"But Katie can and you're too scared to ask her," Violet said as she pulled out of his arms, "Didn't you tell me that you never learn the answer if you don't ask the question?"

"I was talking about you asking your teacher questions if you didn't understand something. This is different." How did he explain that things weren't as simple as they appeared to an eight-year-old?

"Do you want me to ask her for you?" Violet said as she headed toward the back door.

"Violet Louise Maddox, you stop right there before I ground you for the rest of your life."

"Men," his daughter spat out at him as she stomped past him toward her room, looking nothing like the sweet little girl that had gotten up that morning.

His head was spinning. Where had he lost control of this conversation? Maybe where his daughter had thrown her mother's betrayal at him?

Violet had only been seven when her mother had left. There hadn't been a way to explain to her that before she'd even been born he had asked her mother to stay. And he would never share with his daughter how her mother had laughed at him before explaining that she'd had her fill of living on his little houseboat. There were bigger and better places to see out in the world. She needed more excitement than he and his little island could give her.

But Katie wasn't Lilly. Katie would never leave her child so she could roam the world looking for excitement. But could she ever be happy here? With just him and Lilly? Without the bright lights of New York City?

What if Violet was right? What if he let Katie walk away from them without him asking her to stay?

One thing his daughter was absolutely right about: if he didn't ask the question, he would never know the answer.

He found himself walking from room to room. Trying to work out what he needed to do until finally it hit him. Rushing down the hall, he opened his daughter's door only to find that she'd cried herself to sleep.

"Violet, wake up," he said, brushing his hand across his daughter's hair, "I have a plan, but I'm going to need your help."

Katie stood in the middle of Duval Street, dressed in a short emerald dress of lace and silk, and tried to balance on the three-inch heels Jo and Summer had insisted would be perfect for their last night out together.

"There you are" Dylan came up beside her. Dressed in a black three-piece suit, he looked more like a banker than a paramedic.

"Where're Jo and Summer?" she asked as she took the glass of champagne he held out to her. This was supposed to be a girls-only night. The two women had a lot of explaining to do. They could have at least warned her that Dylan would be here tonight.

"They're around here somewhere," he said. "They'll catch up with us later."

"Why are *you* here tonight?" she asked as they took a path down through the artist and galleries until they came to a stop in front of a small shop that she'd never noticed before. Jo and Summer were nowhere to be seen.

"I'll explain in a minute. There's something I want you to see," Dylan said as he opened a door that led into a room lit with crystal chandeliers.

The only furniture in the room was a glass case that ran across the back wall. As Katie approached the it an old man wrinkled with age stepped out of a back room.

"Dylan, I'm so glad to see you. Is this your Katie?" he asked.

"Katie, this is Peter," Dylan said.

"It's nice to meet you, Peter." She gazed down into the case that held as much sparkly jewelry as Tiffany's, forgetting for a moment that she was waiting for Dylan to explain what was going on. "You have some lovely pieces here."

"Peter was a master jeweler in Cuba before he came to Key West," Dylan said then turned to Peter. "Is it ready?"

"Of course, it is ready," Peter replied. "Come see."

Katie watched as Peter pulled a small black velvet box from under the counter. A delicate ring of diamonds surrounding a round solitaire stone set into a white-gold frame lay in front of her.

"It's beautiful," she said. Her breath caught in her chest.

"A little girl told me today that if I didn't ask the question I would never learn the answer."

"She sounds like a smart girl," Katie said, her voice catching as she watched Dylan take the ring into his hand while her own hands began to shake.

"I think so," he said as he took her hand in his. She felt his hand tremble against hers. "Katherine Lee McGee, will you marry me?"

"I don't understand. You've been so distant. I thought you wanted me to leave." She wiped at the tear spilling down her cheek then pulled her hands up to where her heart was hammering inside her chest.

"Oh, yes, Dylan, there's nothing I want more."

She heard someone knocking on the shop window. Turning around she saw four faces pressed against the glass. Jo, Casey, Summer and Violet waved at them before they all spilled into the room.

Violet tugged on her daddy's jacket then whispered into his ear loud enough for everyone to hear her, "You have to kiss her now."

"I was about to," Dylan whispered back just as loud, "but you interrupted us."

After a very PG-rated kiss, Dylan took Katie into his arms.

She'd come to Key West broken and scared, but with the love and support of this man and these friends, she finally felt whole once more.

EPILOGUE

KATIE STOOD ON the balcony looking out at the lights of the city. Inside the New York ballroom her family and friends were celebrating.

"There you are," her father said as he stepped outside to join her. "You look as pretty as your mother did the day I married her."

Stepping toward him, she did a twirl in the dress of lace and satin that her own mother had worn for her parents' wedding. "The dress was perfect."

When Violet asked to wear it one day, Katie's makeup had almost been ruined.

"Your mother would be so proud of you. As I am."

"Thank you, Daddy," she whispered before kissing his age-roughened cheek. "For this party and especially for not giving Dylan a hard time."

Her father had taken the news that she would be marrying a "beach bum" and moving to Key West better than she'd expected. She had to give some of the credit for that to Violet, who had quickly charmed all the McGee men, though her brothers' approval of Dylan hadn't been as quick to come. They'd all given her husband as hard a time as possible, especially Junior. Whenever Dylan was in sight, he could be heard muttering what a shame it was that his sister had picked a beach bum over one of New York's finest.

"I've got something else for you," her father said as he pulled an envelope out of his pocket. "It's the address you asked for along with the name of an old friend that can help if you need it."

She'd just taken the envelope when Dylan and Violet stepped outside to join them.

"Now if the two of you will excuse us, Violet and I are going to get us another piece of that cake?" her father asked Violet.

Katie waited until they left before handing

the envelope to Dylan, who'd been eyeing it since he'd stepped out.

She waited anxiously while Dylan opened the envelope and studied the letter inside.

"How did he get this?" Dylan asked.

"He pulled some favors and did some investigation on his own. Lilly has been in Chicago for the last two months. My father said there's a name of someone local that could help if you'd like your lawyer to contact them. If we call them tomorrow we could have it all settled by the time we return from our honeymoon."

"I don't know how to thank him," Dylan said as he wrapped his arms around her.

"He did it for us, for our family," Katie said as she leaned her head back against him and took in the New York skyline. "Isn't it beautiful?"

"Beautiful," Dylan murmured as he trailed kisses down her neck. "Regrets?"

She thought of the cottage that waited for them when they returned to Key West, the one where the three of them would make a home together. A home where they'd love and fight and she hoped they would welcome other children. It was more than she could ever have dreamed of.

Turning her back to the city, she whispered against his lips. “Never.”

* * * * *

If you enjoyed this story, check out these other great reads from Deanne Anders

December Reunion in Central Park
The Neurosurgeon’s Unexpected Family
Sarah and the Single Dad
Stolen Kiss with the Single Mum

All available now!